Angela

By

Terry Aldred

ISBN:1519424876
ISBN-13:13:978-1519424877

For Hope, Paige and Caroline. Thank you for giving me the time and support I needed to make this book possible.

I want to also thank Stacie Olson for all her hard work in helping my story to be told.

CONTENTS

PRELUDE

Branches ripped across the boy's face as he raced through the woods. He could now taste the blood pouring from the cut in his cheek. His legs were burning from trying to keep this pace, but he could feel the man, or whatever it was, close behind him. He didn't dare look, knowing that taking his eyes from his path would guarantee a hard fall. He didn't need to look; the tight feeling in his chest and the hair rising on the back of his neck told him all he needed to know. That ... thing ... was just behind him. If he could just make it out of the woods to a parking lot or someplace full of people, he would be safe. He knew there was little chance of achieving that goal, since he was not going in the right direction. Every time he tried to head out, that ... thing ... would cut him off.

The farther he went, the denser the undergrowth became. The dim light from the ending day cast shadows that danced across the ground. It was hard to focus at all with the twilight sun barely making it through the dense leaves of the high trees. It was inevitable: the boy stumbled and his speed faltered just for a moment. Another branch tore across his face and a vise-

1

like grip attached to his shoulder and threw him to the ground. He rolled several times and sprang to his feet. He had never moved so smoothly before and his quick recovery from the fall shocked him.

The boy tried to focus on his pursuer's face, but he could not. It seemed never to be in focus. What he could see of his follower's form was huge. The man stood over six feet tall and was almost as broad. The man's figure reminded the boy of the body builders he would see at the amateur competitions sometimes hosted by his school. He looked around for anything that could help him, but there was nothing, not even a stick to throw. Should he run again? The man was just standing there as if he weren't sure what to do next. Finally, the boy took two steps towards the man, jumped, and kicked out, planting both feet on the man's chest. The man staggered back but only a few steps.

Surprised that he could even do such a thing, the boy took advantage of the distraction to run once again. This time, he was able to head in a direction that would take him out of the woods. If he could just keep up this speed, he might just make it ... He could hear the man running behind him again. How did he catch up so fast? The boy poured on more speed and was finally making some headway. He could still hear his pursuer, but he seemed to be farther behind. He ran for several minutes longer and was too scared to look back. Though it was starting to get dark, he could see the lights from a parking lot just on the other side of the trees. Those lights shone from the general store that his family had owned for years. It was the only place around and bound to be full of people. Tears came to his eyes as he realized that he was going to make it and see his parents again. Then the man suddenly appeared right in front of him! The boy tried to yell, but fear had stripped him of the ability to speak. The man reached out and grabbed him and as he did so, the man's hands changed, forming shackles around the boy's wrists. The boy tried to scream as he felt the pressure on the bones in his arms, but before a word could escape his lips, there was an intense flash of light and they were both gone..

1
ANGELA

"Another morning; augh!" yawned Angela. "I'm up, Mom, I'm up!"

"Don't be late for school again; I'm not driving you today! I have a lot of packing to do and I just don't have the time. Get up!!" yelled her mom.

"I'm getting up, Mom, I won't be late!" Angela yelled as she slid out of bed, knowing perfectly well that she would probably be late.

"You know, if you would just go to bed at a decent hour you wouldn't have so much trouble getting up for school! You have only been in 10th grade for a month, and I'm afraid you are sleeping through it!" returned her mother.

Angela was never one to enjoy getting up for school, and today was no exception. After going to bed well after 2:00 in the morning for four days in a row, getting up at 6:30 was no easy feat. If it weren't for the weekend, where her mom would graciously allow her to sleep until 10:00, Angela would probably never make it to school. She couldn't help it; she was a night owl. She didn't seem to come to her senses until well after 8:00 every night. The morning was just not for her.

Angela shuffled to her closet and decided on her outfit for the day. Her mom would make her clean her room on occasion, when it needed it, but the closet was hers. It could be as messy as she wanted it. There was no need to open the closet door; the contents had crept far enough out into the room that the door no longer closed. To the untrained eye, the closet looked like a total mess, but she had a system that allowed her to find anything she needed quickly.

When Angela and her mother had moved into this house, Angela was allowed to decorate it any way she liked. Angela focused on greens and browns, and she loved her room. Her mother was quite an artist, so Angela had asked her to paint a mural on the wall. It took several weeks, but the result was everything that Angela had hoped it would be. Behind her bed was the trunk of a huge oak tree, with branches full of big green leaves that grew into and across both adjoining walls. Flying through the trees were birds of all different colors. Her double bed had four small posts and a white sheer canopy covering it on three sides. Along with her dresser and desk was a small night table by the bedside. The detail in the mural was amazing, and sometimes, her mom would surprise her and add another bird to the tree. When Angela opened her window to allow the breeze to caress her room, she could almost imagine that she was in that tree. On the wall opposite the tree above her desk were dozens of photos taped or tacked to the wall. Angela loved to take photographs and had many cameras to prove it.

After Angela got dressed for the day, she watched her mom running around and packing everything she could fit into one suitcase and a carry-on.

"What time does your flight leave again?" asked Angela as she collapsed into a kitchen chair.

As with many families, Angela and her mom spent the most amount of time in their kitchen. The room was just big enough for the two of them, and her mother added her own flair to the room soon after they moved in. The old striped wall paper was torn down, the walls were painted yellow, and the peach cabinets were repainted white. Angela and her mom couldn't imagine why anyone would paint cabinets peach. Ivy stencils ringed the ceiling and came down across the cabinet faces and the door pulls were all replaced with pulls shaped like daisies. With cut flowers on every counter and an old pine table at the far end, the refinished room reminded Angela of a picnic every time she ate in it.

"Didn't we have this conversation yesterday morning?" Angela's mother said with a smile. "My flight leaves at 10:30; I have just enough time to get some toast in you and finish up my packing. With the security process at the airport, I am going to need every minute. Are you sure you are going to be okay? It's not too late to call your uncle; you can spend the time with him and your cousins," said her mom.

"Mom, I am old enough to spend a few days on my own, and if I need Uncle Andy he is only ten minutes away. Besides, I know you told him to check in on me anyway," said Angela.

"It's not a few days and you know it. It's a week!" replied her mom.

Angela was right: her mom had arranged for her Uncle Andy to check in during the week, even though she knew that

Angela was old enough to take care of herself. Angela already did most of the cooking and cleaning, since her mother needed to work to support the two of them. Ever since Angela's father had passed away from cancer, Angela had been forced to grow up more quickly than her mother would have liked. At the time of her father's death, Angela was given a great deal of attention by people that she didn't really know. She was never comfortable with that attention because she knew that they didn't understand what she was going through or how much she loved and missed her father. That attention made Angela more comfortable being away from the limelight and by herself. She much preferred to be settled in the background and not the center of attention. She did not draw herself away from the world, but became more of an observer. Angela found that observation made for a perfect place from which to take a picture. Angela took the sorrow of her loss and expressed it through her photographs. She had a gift of seeing the true beauty of any scene and capturing it brilliantly in a photo, be it digital or print. Even knowing how capable Angela was of caring for herself, her mother was still nervous due to the story that had been on the news over the last few weeks.

"Well, as long as you're sure. I'm just so nervous about that story on TV about all those kids disappearing. I know most of them were far from here, but I am still nervous... my goodness, Angela, look at you! You're a mess. I imagine you went to bed later than you should have again. I don't know how you stand on two feet."

"Come on, Mom, I have heard this before. I'm fine and I will still be fine while you're away!" sighed Angela. She had to admit that she cornered the market on the disheveled look, but as the day grew on she always seemed to pull it together.

Angela was a pretty girl, but it was hard to see her beauty with the dark shadows under her eyes. She was not fond of the sun, since she burned easily, so she preferred to stay out of it. As a result, her skin, although blemish-free, had almost a white glow. She had dark brown hair that she liked to keep long because she hated going to get it cut. She also had light blue eyes that sparkled when she smiled. Not one for skirts, dresses, or any of the latest clothing fads, her wardrobe contained mostly jeans and sweatshirts. Unfortunately, no matter what she did, she always looked tired, due to her late-night tendencies, and school did not cater to her night-time addiction. She was very smart and absorbed information easily; that was, when she could stay awake long enough to listen. She always thought that a night school would be her best option, but that didn't exist in this little town. She tried coffee before school to help keep herself alive during the first few periods, but that only lasted an hour and then soon after she was really tired. Her mom was not fond of the coffee option either. Angela could still remember that "You're too young" and, "You just need more sleep" speech pretty clearly. So, Angela did the best she could with her subjects and tried to hold it together until the night time.

"You're only going to be away for a few days. I will keep things together here and you can take your class without any worries," said Angela.

Angela's mom worked for the small insurance company in town. She was good at her job, so her agency promoted her and signed her up for a class at their home office in Tennessee.

"Of course I'm going to worry, and it's not a few days, it's still a week!" The stress in her mom's face finally relaxed as she looked at how grown up her daughter had become. With love in her eyes, Angela's mom said, "You know I have every confidence in you, and I know you will be fine. Now, I put a list of important numbers on the fridge. If you need anything at all, call your Uncle Andy. I left $200 in the coupon drawer for food and whatever else comes up. Don't go spending it on photography equipment. I don't need you eating peanut butter all week because you bought another camera!"

Angela's photography class was the one class she had no problems focusing in. Her portfolio was very robust, but it was clear that her favorite photos were black and white. Not always depending on digital prints, she had a small darkroom in her basement at home. Many sleepless nights were spent down there experimenting with several types of exposures and paper, always going for the perfect photo to add to her collection. Angela took at least one camera everywhere she went, and she had enough cameras that she could take a different one with her every day for two weeks. She said that each one had its own personality and the photos each camera took reflected that personality. Not many people understood that point of view, but one thing they did all agree on was that she had an eye for a great photo. Most of Angela's friends had iPods filled with music; she had one filled with her photos.

Angela was already thinking about what piece of camera equipment she could get with that $200, and how she didn't really mind peanut butter, when her Mom said, as if she were reading Angela's thoughts, "I want to see receipts from the grocery store when I get back!"

"What? Don't you trust me, Mom?" Angela replied with a sly grin on her face.

"Of course I do. I trust you to go buy a camera and live on saltines and pop tarts for five days; that's why I want to see receipts!" grinned her mom. "Now eat your breakfast before it gets too late."

Angela and her mom lived in a small home in Pennsylvania, about three hours outside of Philadelphia, in a town called Gap. Though the house looked like most of the other houses in their neighborhood, they had both added their own personalities to each of the rooms and those changes made the house home for them. Her mom's paintings and Angela's photos were all over the house. Neither Angela's nor her mom's work centered on any one theme; the subjects of the photos and paintings varied greatly from one to the next. When Angela's mom saw something she liked, she painted it, and when Angela saw something she liked, she took its picture.

The family used to live in Minnesota, but Angela's mom had had to find a new job after her husband died. Angela's Uncle Andy lived here in Gap and was able to find Angela's mother a job. It was a difficult move from Minnesota, but her uncle was here and he helped them get settled.

Even though it was only three hours from Philadelphia, Gap was still a pretty rural area, similar to where they had lived in Minnesota. That similarity really helped with the adjustment of moving from Minnesota. There were not as many wide open places in Gap as there were back home in Minnesota, but the local forests and parks were really appealing to Angela. So much so, that Angela was fond of all the walks through the woods near her home. Angela and her mom lived very close to state game lands, so there were acres and acres of woods to explore, enjoy, and, best of all, photograph. Many of Angela's photos had won contests at various levels. Her mom was convinced that Angela would become a famous photographer. Angela believed the photographer part, but not so much the famous part.

One strange fact about Angela was that she liked to walk through the woods when the moon was high and the leaves on all the trees took on a silver color. She was never scared walking alone at night, but instead felt more alive than ever. She loved how the starlight cut through the trees as she walked, and how the moon would cast a glow that would light the entire woods. Angela's friends and her mom never understood the attraction nighttime held for her, but in a strange way nighttime seemed to bring Angela closer to the memories she had of her father. He loved the nighttime too, and she felt that he moved into the night when he died. Nighttime was where she could feel like she was with him again. She would tell her mom that the woods at night were very different than during the day, so much so, that they could have been from a different land. Her mom still didn't get it.

In the warm kitchen, Angela smiled and focused on the toast that was in her hand. She knew how obsessive her mom could be and figured it would be best to buy food and see about a new camera when her mom got home. Still very tired, she had zoned out while ignoring her toast when her mom said, "Hey, day dreamer." That's what her mom called her when she was 'sleeping with her eyes open,' another one of her mom's famous quotes. "It's time to catch the bus...hold on, hold on," she said as Angela bolted out of the room, "Take this piece of toast, and give me a hug. I will call you when I get there, and don't forget to buy food!"

Angela hugged her mom and said with a smile, "You have a good time at your class and try to learn something! I will be fine here." As she crossed the front lawn, she glanced back over at her house. She thought about how comfortable her mom had made their home. She still thought of the house as "new," even though they had been there for three years. Her neighbors were all very nice and had been very helpful when they first moved in. The house sat just far enough away from

Angela's school that it took a good walk to get there, so getting out in time for the bus was her best option.

Today was a good day. Angela arrived at the bus stop just as the bus was coming around the corner. "Wow, and a Monday, even!" said the bus driver. Angela smiled in that sarcastic way that only a teenager could, and headed toward her seat. Another indication of a good day was that only one projectile hit her before she could sit down.

"At least it wasn't wet," said Natalie, "and look at you all here on a Monday!"

"Is everyone a comedian today?" asked Angela, as she removed the paper ball from her hair and sat down. Angela hated the bus, the spit ball fights, the loud music and, worst of all, the smell. It was a typical yellow bus with the uncomfortable olive green seats and the wonderful fragrance that seemed like a mix of old stinky lunches and dirty sweat socks. The busses where she used to live had smelled the same way. She figured they bottled that school bus smell and sprayed it inside to make all kids equally miserable all across the country. At least she had gotten a seat today. There had been many times, mostly on the way home, that she had to crowd into an already full seat because there were no open seats left. Today, not only did she have a seat, she got to sit with Natalie.

Natalie was one of Angela's few friends. Though she was a tiny little girl, she talked enough for two people. Her favorite words were, "I know, right?" With long straight blond hair, she was very pretty, but tended to talk herself into most of her problems. Few people had enough patience to tolerate her. Angela didn't mind; she was able to tune Natalie out when she needed a break, and hold onto enough of the conversation to nod in all the appropriate places. This time, Natalie said something that brought Angela right back into the real world.

"Did you hear that another kid disappeared?" asked Natalie.

"What did you say? There was another disappearance?" asked Angela.

"Yeah," said Natalie, looking up with her huge blue eyes. "He went to Morgan, can you believe it?" continued Natalie. Morgan High was one of their rival schools. "The same as the last one: he went to school and sometime after lunch he was just gone. The weird thing is this school isn't like ours. They have security cameras all over and they saw him go into the locker rooms and then he never came out. They had teachers and cops looking everywhere. They even had trained dogs looking for him, but he just disappeared. What do you think happened?" asked Natalie.

"I have no idea, but it does seem strange that no one saw him," answered Angela.

"I know, right? I mean to just disappear like that is crazy. Everyone's parents are freaking out. I mean, just look at the bus."

Angela hadn't really noticed at first, but Natalie was right. There were only two more stops before they arrived at school, and the bus was half as full as it usually was by this time. Angela was glad her Mom had not heard the news or she never would have left for her class. It wasn't that Angela was looking forward to her mom leaving, it was just that her mom worked very hard and was really looking forward to this class. For the last three weeks, she had been talking about nothing else. It would be good for her to get away for a few days and not have to worry that her daughter was going to disappear.

"This one is a little close to home, if you ask me," replied Angela.

"I know, right?" answered Natalie.

After that, Natalie started talking about a myriad of things, none of which Angela really paid attention to. She couldn't stop thinking about the poor kids that had disappeared; at least until the spit ball hit her in the side of the face.

"I hate the bus," sighed Angela

"That one did look pretty wet," Natalie said with a grin.

The bus continued and the spit balls flew. At least today Angela was not the main target; she was more like collateral damage. Sometimes, the battle cry 'Fire!' was followed by a flurry of spit and paper and on one particularly bad day ... that cry had been followed by gum.

When the bus finally arrived and everyone filed off, Angela's thoughts were still on the lost boy. It was strange that it was really affecting her. Perhaps it was just the jitters about her mom leaving.

"So, Angela, when's the party this week with your mom away and all?" asked Natalie.

"No, no, no! My mom would flip!" exclaimed Angela.

"Don't worry; it will be a small party," Natalie said with a smile, as she wandered off towards her homeroom.

Before Angela could say anything else, she heard a voice come from behind her. "Hey, loser!" Angela cringed. She was hoping not to have to deal with this today.

"Hello ... Jane." Angela turned to see Jane sauntering over with her posse.

Everyone knows a Jane Crawford; the beautiful, popular girl in school who knows it, and likes to let others know it as well. The clothes, the hair, the bling; Jane has it all. She is so used to getting what she wants, that now she expects nothing less. That's Jane on the outside. On the inside, Jane is alone. She has the people that she calls friends, but they don't really want to be her friend, they want to be her. At least they want to be the 'her' that they see. When Jane goes home, there are people there to make sure she has what she wants, but her parents are seldom involved. They had a child because it was the thing to do at the time, but now their own personal wants and desires have taken them in different directions. Occasionally, they cross paths in the evening between a function, event, or gathering, but all Jane shows them is scorn, the scorn that she has felt for too many years now. What is left is now anger. It is that anger that keeps her from feeling alone, but it is an anger she now shares with others - especially with those that are devoid of that anger.

"So, loser, what are you taking pictures of today? There's some overflowing garbage cans over there; maybe that would be nice."

"That WOULD be nice. Maybe you could pose in front of it for me; you could all add some color."

"Ha, ha," Jane said, as she sauntered past. "That spit ball in your hair looks nice, by the way." Two of the "sparkle girls," as Angela calls them due to all the sparkle makeup they wear, bumped into her as they walked by. The funny thing was, even after three years, she still didn't know their names.

The garbage can comment was not far off the mark. Angela loved taking unique pictures and could take a great picture no matter what the subject matter was. She wouldn't put it past herself to take a "garbage shot" now and again if she saw something in it.

As tired as she usually was, homeroom tended to be a blur to Angela. She didn't spend much time there and she sat with all the people whose last names started with L through N. The announcements today seemed to go on and on and finally the bell rang for first period history. The problem with history was that she really didn't wake up until second period and because of that it was Angela's worst subject. She actually really liked history. It was rare that she made it to school early enough to go, and when she did make it, she found that it was just too hard to pay attention that early in the morning. None of her friends were in the class, either, so that did not help when it came to staying awake. In addition to trying to keep her eyes open, Angela was not fond of Mr. Myers. He was boring and slow and did nothing to make his class even remotely interesting.

Second period was English, and by then, Angela could actually function. Natalie was in that class with her, so the constant chatter helped to bring her out of her fog as well. It also helped that it was taught by one of her favorite teachers, Mrs. Wren. Mrs. Wren loved to decorate her classroom. There were posters and quotes and some of Angela's own photographs decorating the walls. There were also framed copies of all the yearbooks going back several years all on one large wall. Angela often wondered what all the people in those books were doing now, knowing that they had all started here.

Mrs. Gloria Wren was a model teacher. After twenty years in the classroom, she had seen it all. Every type of kid had passed through her doors, and she saw something good in each one. But there were some that really outshone the others. She knew that she shouldn't have any favorites, but sometimes she couldn't help it. Her favorites were the kids that just lit up the room when they walked in. They might not be the most talkative or the smartest, but they had something special about them that left a mark on all those who crossed their paths.

Some kids were even terrible trouble makers, but sometimes it was those kids who surprised her the most in later years. Mrs. Wren was deeply into nostalgia; she loved to keep track of everything and everyone. She had a copy of every yearbook that the school had ever published. She also kept track of newspaper clippings mentioning her students. She kept in touch with as many former students as she could, and was fond of finding out what paths many of them had taken. Having no family of her own, she had taken it upon herself to adopt those whom she had taught and, in a sense, built a family of her own. She definitely included Angela in that family.

"Good morning, class. I can see you're all excited for another week of school. I want to remind you that today is the first day for the yearbook committee. We will be meeting here after school," said Mrs. Wren.

"I completely forgot about that today," whispered Angela.

"I know, right?" replied Natalie. "I assume that you are going to take pictures again this year?"

"I am; they are not my favorite pictures to take, but I know Mrs. Wren really wants me to come back. It also doesn't hurt my English grade," Angela whispered, with a smile.

"Girls, is there something you wish to share with the class?" Mrs. Wren said while standing just behind them.

"No, Mrs. Wren," answered both girls in unison with a sing song voice.

After an hour of analyzing *Taming the Shrew*, third period began. As with history, Angela was not close to any people in her geometry class. What helped pass the time was that she was really good at it. She was able to visualize shapes and angles in her head as well as anyone could with paper. Mr. Hess was her geometry teacher. He had a good heart and

Angela liked how encouraging he could be. He always pushed his students to do well, and he never came down on Angela for looking so tired. He accepted people for who they were and seldom passed any judgments. He was an all-around good teacher.

Next period was gym...let's just say that Angela is good at math.

Finally, fifth period came: lunch. This was Angela's time to catch up with her friends. Stepping into the cafe, the strong smell of bleach hit her, just as it did every other day. The far wall was an outside wall and lined with windows that looked down into the valley. Angela loved that view. Sometimes she felt as if she could launch herself out of those windows and fly over the neighboring houses. From the kitchen, the sweet smell of tomato sauce hit her nose and her stomach growled. 'Pizza Day,' she thought. The tables were set up in rows with the round little stools that were built into the table; they were very uncomfortable. If you could get to the cafe early enough, you could grab one of those high tables with the real seats. Emma's last class was just next door to the cafeteria, and she was often able to do just that.

When Angela moved into the area back when she was thirteen, the first person she met was Emma. Angela never forgot that meeting. She had just been starting to get into photography. Her mom had bought her a new camera as a little bribe for moving, so she decided to wander out and see the new area and take some pictures. After a bit of meandering, she found her way to a playground. Instead of wood chips covering the ground, it had pieces of recycled tires spread all around, which gave you a little spring in your step as you walked. On this particular day, there were not too many people around, but there was plenty to photograph. The playground was nestled in a small wooded area in the corner of the park. The trees helped keep the area very cool, but at the same time they made the playground very secluded. The light shone through onto the bars of the different playground pieces, making excellent shadows and lines for photos. Being secluded, the playground also made a nice hangout for any local bullies. As Angela approached with her eyes in her viewfinder, she inadvertently bumped into the wrong kid. Before she could react, her new camera was grabbed out of her hands.

"Hey, give that back!" yelled Angela.

"Make me," said the boy. He had two of his toadies by his side.

"That is my camera and I want it back now!" yelled Angela again.

"OOOHHH," teased one of the toadies.

Angela approached the boy with her camera and tried to grab it, but he was too quick. Covered with acne, and cursed with an unpleasant smell that seemed to be a combination of body odor and greasy hair, the boy sneered at Angela. Again, Angela made a grab for the camera, but the boy tossed it to one of his friends.

"Give it here," said Angela, approaching the small little weasel.

"No way. I think we're going to keep it," he said, as he tossed it back to the leader.

As Angela turned to chase after the camera, the other sidekick stuck out his foot and Angela tripped. She didn't fall, but the stumble brought about more laughing from the gang and more embarrassment for Angela.

"That's enough, Roy," said a voice from somewhere behind her. It wasn't an adult. That was plain, but the voice had a confident authority behind it.

"Give the camera back."

"This doesn't concern you, Emma," sneered the leader, whose name had to be Roy.

Angela took advantage of the distraction and grabbed for the camera. Taken off guard, Roy pushed at Angela, and she fell to the ground. Emma was right there and taller than all three boys. When Roy turned to push Emma, she grabbed his hand, twisted his palm up and bent it at the wrist back towards him so his fingers were pointed straight up in the air. The immediate pain made Roy yell. Emma then took her other hand and forced Roy's distorted hand towards his body, putting more pressure on his wrist. Emma performed her move with practiced deliberateness, and the shock and pain of the move showed clearly on Roy's face as he fell to his knees and screamed in pain. One of Roy's toadies went to move towards Emma, but the look of determination on her face, coupled with the tears of pain on Roy's, was enough to keep him at bay. The third boy saw what he was up against and knew what would happen to his reputation when he was beaten by a girl. He decided that it was suddenly time to go home for dinner. Still applying pressure to Roy's wrist with her right hand, Emma reached down with her left, and gently removed the camera from Roy's other hand.

Quietly, but still loud enough for Roy and Angela to hear, Emma said, "Next time, you should think twice before you decide to take something that does not belong to you," and as quick as a shot, she placed her foot against his chest, pushed, and sent him sprawling onto his back. Looking around, Emma saw that the second boy had already extracted himself from the scene. Knowing that he was alone, Roy decided that a silent tactical retreat was best. Angela got up and turned to take a look at her new friend.

Emma was taller than Angela, with long brown hair and glasses. She had pretty hazel eyes and a bearing that exuded confidence. She wore jeans and a sweat shirt that was perhaps a size too big.

"That was impressive!' said Angela. "Where did you learn to do that!? My name is Angela."

"Thanks, Angela! My dad teaches self-defense classes at the Y. My name's Emma. That is a nice camera. Is it new?"

"Thanks. It is a new camera. Let me show you how it works," said Angela, noticing how interested Emma seemed.

Throughout the rest of the day, Emma and Angela took pictures of everything. Ever since then, they had been the best of friends.

"Hey, Angela," smiled Emma. "How was gym today?"

"Dodge ball," replied Angela succinctly, as she collapsed in her chair with her tray.

"Owwww. Enough said about that! Don't let it get you down, though, we have yearbook today. That should be fun," answered Emma.

Just as Angela was about to comment about the yearbook meeting, another one of their friends dropped noisily beside Emma. "Hi, Pete," said Natalie. Pete and Natalie had been dating off and on for two years. Right now, Angela was not sure if it was an off time or an on time, so she was careful not to bring it up.

"Did you guys hear about the kid that disappeared? Practically in our back yard, too! This whole thing creeps me out, if you ask me," said Pete.

"I try not to think about it. I don't even like to put the news on any more. I'm afraid that I might see someone I know," added Emma. "Especially you, Angela, the way you like to wander at night."

"I don't wander," rebuked Angela.

"Really? And what do you call it?" returned Emma sternly.

"It's no different than what everyone else does during the day, except I do it at night. I love the woods at night time. And besides, everyone seemed to have disappeared in broad daylight in areas that have tons of people," returned Angela.

"That's what makes this really disturbing. If someone disappears walking home late at night when no one is around, then you think that if you avoid that situation, you probably will be fine. What makes this situation hard is that kids are disappearing from places most people think are safe. That one kid went missing from a church!" said Pete.

"I know, right? My mom knows someone whose cousin is the mother of the kid that disappeared this time," chattered Natalie.

"She knows the cousin of the mother who is the son ... who is... huh?" said Pete with a smile. Pete was a really good guy, but not the sharpest tool in the shed.

"Never mind. What Natalie's saying is that the last kid who disappeared is not a nameless face on the TV. The next one could be someone we know. What is it up to, six lost kids now?" asked Angela.

"Something like that," answered Natalie.

Emma looked at Angela with worry in her eyes.

"I still wish you could stay in at night until this blows over," said Emma.

Angela wanted to respond, but didn't know what to say. Her entire body and soul felt better at night and she wasn't sure she could give that up. Angela chose not to say anything, and looked at her fork as though it was the first time she had seen one.

"Well, I know how to keep her in at least this Friday. Sleepover!" said Natalie. "Angela's mom is not going to be home and that gives us all Friday night and most of Saturday to hang out!"

"I'm in!" yelled Pete.

"I don't think so!" scolded Emma.

"Had to try. I'm going to get some lunch." With that remark, Pete got up to head for the lunch line.

"A sleepover sounds better than a party," replied Angela. "My mom told me that I could have a sleep over this weekend if I got lonely."

"Uh oh, don't look now, but here come Jane and the 'wanna-bees.' Maybe if we don't make eye contact they will go away," Natalie laughed.

"Look who we have here! All these losers in one place. I think they may be spreading," said Jane.

"What's that smell?" said Emma, in a distracted tone. "I don't think it's my sandwich. Did someone step in... oh, wait, Jane's here. Hi, Jane."

"Very funny, loser. We have come to tell you the good news."

"You're leaving the school?" said Emma.

With a scornful look, Jane continued, "We decided that you are in need of our direction."

"And what direction could you possibly give us?" said Angela.

"On the yearbook, of course. We are tired of you losers running the yearbook, so we are getting involved to give you direction. See you at the meeting," returned Jane as she led her squad away.

"She can't be serious," said Emma, as Jane and her followers left the cafeteria.

"Great," said Angela. "That is the last thing we need. So much for looking forward to yearbook today."

"For some reason, I'm just not hungry anymore," said Natalie.

"No worries. I'll eat that," said Pete as he returned and reached over for Natalie's sandwich.

After lunch, the girls and Pete headed off on their separate ways. Angela and Emma began to head to photography. As they passed the common room, Angela thought she saw something out of the corner of her eye. Just a flicker, but it was definitely something.

When she turned to look, Emma asked, "What is it?"

"I'm not sure. I thought I saw something, but I don't see... I must be tired," she said.

"I didn't see anything," returned Emma. "What camera did you bring today?"

From there, the conversation stayed on cameras. As far as Angela was concerned, her entire day led to this one class. She had had a love for photography ever since her father bought her that first camera, and her teacher, Ms. Cray, had been a great influence on the quality of her photos. Angela and Ms. Cray hit it off on day one. They both moved into the area at the same time, so they shared their first day of school together. Ms. Cray had long black hair and loved big, billowy, colorful clothes; sweaters and peasant tops were her favorites. She also had a fluffy black feather boa that she often wore to class. Ms. Cray's dark, black glasses with big clear rhinestones in each corner often caught the light just right and cast rainbows in various spots of the room. Those glasses fit her long slender face and dark green eyes well. Ms. Cray stood a little taller than Angela, and although she seemed to have a slight build, there were times when Angela could tell or almost sense that Ms. Cray was strong for her size. Angela had always thought Ms. Cray was very pretty, and guessed that she was either in her late twenties or early thirties. Ms. Cray's classroom was filled with little bobbles, trinkets, and collectables that were all brightly colored and flashy. Though Ms. Cray said that she kept those trinkets around for students to take pictures of, Angela had caught her admiring them on more than one occasion. Angela liked that about her favorite teacher. Angela and Ms. Cray spent many hours after school talking about everything while they developed and printed all the pictures they had taken. They had similar tastes in the type of photos they liked, too, and often couldn't remember who had taken which photo. As time progressed, Angela's and Ms. Cray's relationship moved from a 'teacher/student' relationship to more of a 'mentor/protégé' relationship, until they finally became just good friends.

When Angela and Emma got to class, Ms. Cray had not yet arrived. Without wasting any time, they got out their cameras and started to collect their equipment for the day's work. Photography met in the old chemistry room. The room didn't have any desks, but three long tables spread across the room in three rows. The students sat at the tables, and each student was assigned a row of drawers that were built into the tables. Five or six students could sit at each table and still have plenty of room to work. It was sometimes a hassle when you had to move all the way around the table to photograph the other side of an object, since you had to walk all the way around the outside of the room, but the drawers were packed full of film and other supplies for all the students. At one end of each table there was also a working sink. Angela was always surprised by the budget Ms. Cray had for her class. Ms. Cray seemed always to have an unlimited supply of the best photography equipment and computers for her students. Angela and Emma sat at the front table, nearest to Ms. Cray's desk.

With all the items in the room available to photograph, it was sometimes hard to pick out a subject for the day's pictures. This day, Angela chose a black and white flower vase. She was working on black and whites today and decided that the vase would give her photograph interesting shades of grey. Emma was working on shadows, so she chose a variety of items of different heights and a number of different light sources, so she would have many shadows that overlapped at several angles. As they were setting up, Ms. Cray came in to the room, all excited.

"Girls, check out my new shoes!" exclaimed Ms. Cray. She didn't seem to try to hide that Angela and Emma were her favorite students.

"What are those?!" laughed Angela.

"I saw those in a magazine. Are they comfortable?" asked Emma.

Looking down at Ms. Cray's feet, Emma saw the strangest shoes she had ever laid eyes on. They looked like grey running shoes, but each individual toe was carved out. It basically looked like she had wrapped her foot in sneaker material.

"Do you have socks on in there?" asked Angela, laughing.

"Sure do. They look just like the shoe, with a spot for each of my toes," answered Ms. Cray, as she wiggled her toes through the fabric.

"I think they are the coolest thing," said Emma, "but aren't they running shoes?"

"They are," replied Ms. Cray.

"When do you go running?" asked Emma, with a gleam in her eye.

"Only when someone is chasing me!" laughed Ms. Cray as she moved to her desk, "Okay, class, let's get started on today's projects."

"I like Ms. Cray, but she can be a little crazy," said Emma

"I agree, but that is one of the things I like the most about her," answered Angela with a smile.

Class continued, with each of the students working on their projects for the day. Angela was engrossed in her photography, as always. Her vase was working well as a subject and she took many pictures at several different angles. She then decided to add another object, to give some contrast to the vase. She wandered around the room wondering what would work best. Along the window sills were several different objects. First, she picked up a snow globe that held what looked like a Las Vegas casino. She liked the absurdity of the idea of snow in Vegas, but the globe was too small. A figurine of a cow wearing a sparkly hat and sunglasses didn't fit at all. From there, Angela saw a small green rock. At least she thought it was a rock; it was like a quartz crystal but green. The rock was narrow like a pencil or pen, but only two inches long. Angela knew it would not work in her picture, but she was curious about the stone and liked how pretty it looked as the sun filtered through its facets. Angela reached down to pick up the stone and as it settled in her palm, she noticed a slight tingle. Before she could react, a shot of electricity moved through her arm and straight into her chest. With a startled gasp of pain, she dropped the stone back onto the window sill. A few people turned her way, but then quickly returned back to their pictures. Angela didn't notice her teacher staring at her with a confused look on her face. Though the pain subsided quickly, Angela didn't know what to make of it. She stood quietly for a moment, then noticed for the first time that there were only five minutes left in class. Angela decided that she had taken enough photos for the day and went to straighten up her area.

"You okay?" asked Emma. "Your face is all pale."

"I don't know what happened. I touched that rock over there and it shocked me!" answered Angela. When she turned to look back over at the rock, though, it was gone.

"What rock?" asked Emma.

"That's funny. There was a green rock right over there a second ago. It must have fallen onto the floor."

Just then, the bell rang for the end of class.

"Before you go, class, don't forget that your homework project this week is people pictures. I want them developed and on my desk by Friday," said Ms. Cray, as her students shuffled out the door.

"Come on," said Emma. "We can't be late for health class again or Whipple will kill us."

Angela turned to say good bye to Ms. Cray, but the teacher had disappeared into the dark room behind her desk. Grabbing the rest of her things, Angela followed Emma to their last class of the day: Health, with Mr. Whipple.

Although Emma and Angela had their health class together, they didn't sit near each other. Mr. Whipple's class was given seating assignments from day one, arranged by alphabetical order according to last name. This organization put Angela on one side of the room and Emma smack in the middle. Many different health-oriented posters decorated the classroom, some showing the basic food groups, others showing pictures of various anatomical subjects. Mr. Whipple was fond of the "Eat This Not That" books, so many posters with that subject matter could be found hanging around the class as well. Like many classrooms, Mr. Whipple's had a large bookshelf with an extensive library. The subjects varied, but many of his books naturally focused on medicine and health. However, he also had some war-related books and even a section on hobbies like fly fishing. Few people borrowed those books, but Mr. Whipple strongly advocated getting outdoors and enjoying the day. He often said getting outdoors was one of the best things you could do for yourself. In his classroom, texting or passing notes was strictly forbidden, and the slightest infraction of class rules was rewarded with a detention that always involved cleaning something with a toothbrush. Not wanting to miss the yearbook meeting that afternoon, Angela and Emma were careful not to earn the 'Wrath of Whipple,' another Gap High phrase, and did not attempt to text each other.

By the end of the class, Angela's arm still felt sore. She flexed her hand many times, trying to get the numbness to go away, when Mr. Whipple approached her.

"Something wrong with your arm, Angela?" asked Mr. Whipple.

"I'm not sure. It feels all tingly," answered Angela.

"Let me see. Extend your arm all the way out and turn your palm up. Hold on. What's that on your hand? It looks like a small electrical burn," observed Mr. Whipple. "Did you touch something electrical?"

Angela wasn't sure she was ready to try to explain the stone. "I was messing around with one of my old cameras in photography class, changing around the battery packs. I don't remember the packs giving me a shock, but I can't imagine what else would have done it."

Mr. Whipple wasn't convinced by Angela's explanation, but he was used to getting strange explanations from students that didn't ring entirely true. He knew Angela well enough to know that if she were not telling the truth, she had a good enough reason for it.

"Okay. Well, if the tingling doesn't go away by the end of the day, you should have it checked out. I can give you something for the burn, though." He went into his desk and pulled out a bandage and some cream. After putting the cream on the Band-aid, he applied it to the burn.

"That feels better already. Thank you," said Angela

"No problem. Keep an eye on that arm," answered Mr. Whipple.

Soon after their conversation, the class bell rang. Angela and Emma had study hall for the last period of the day. Each student had the option of staying in their classroom for study hall, or spending the time in the library. Emma was not in Angela's study hall class, but they always met in the library.

Mrs. Boyd was the school librarian, and she was as typical a librarian as you could get. She was very strict on her rules for being quiet, but also quick to help a student who was interested in using the library for research. The library was a much bigger space than was usual in most high schools. A wealthy local resident had passed away a few years previously, and donated enough money to the school to give it a state-of-the-art library. The donation included a grant for a very sophisticated computer system and a huge expansion, so there were plenty of places Angela and Emma could go to be alone. Occasionally, Mrs. Boyd would appear out of nowhere to shush them, but mostly they could talk quietly without interruption.

As the two of them sat down, Emma noticed the Band-aid on Angela's palm.

"How is your hand?" asked Emma.

"It's still a little tingly. Mr. Whipple gave me some cream for the burn and told me to keep an eye on my arm. I can picture my mom freaking out if I call her from the emergency room for any reason; she would turn around and come back on the next plane!"

"I'm sure you will be fine," assured Emma.

"Me, too," replied Angela, but she wasn't really sure. Her arm did still feel strange. She had received an electrical shock once before, so she knew what a shock felt like. One day when unplugging a lamp in her room, her finger inadvertently touched the plug prongs before they had completely left the socket. The jolt was not severe, but it certainly let her know that she shouldn't have touched the cord end. The pain felt the same as today's pain, but back then the tingling had been gone within a few minutes. Now, it had been over an hour since she picked up the green stone, and it almost felt as though the tingling was going farther up her arm into her shoulder. It didn't exactly hurt, but it was definitely a strange feeling.

"Friday should be fun," said Emma, bringing Angela out of her train of thought.

"What? Oh, yeah, it should be. You do remember that there is little sleeping when Natalie is around! Last time she spent the night, she talked non-stop until well past 2:00! We will have to listen in shifts!" laughed Angela.

"Girls, be quiet back there," shushed Mrs. Boyd

With a grin, Emma and Angela went back to their homework.

2

THE STONE

The group that worked on the yearbook met in the common room outside of Mrs. Wren's class. The common room was a large room that stood in the center of the school and opened to the main hallway that ringed the school. The common room contained several tables with computers that anyone could use whenever they needed more space or computer time. Many of the kids that were on the yearbook staff also worked on the recently created school paper called "Bridging the Gap." Angela always thought that was a crafty name, considering the name of her school.

When the group entered the room, Mrs. Wren was finishing some work, so most of the kids walked around and caught up with friends they had not seen recently; some texted friends they didn't see at all. Angela took the opportunity to take some photos of the people in the room. Some smiled as she clicked away, and some ignored her. Those were the shots she liked the best. Sometimes she wished she could be an invisible observer who could move around people without ever being noticed. Everyone could smile for a picture, but rarely could you capture someone's true essence in a photo when they wore a big goofy grin and had someone behind them making rabbit ears above their head. The photos where people were truly being themselves and not paying any attention to the camera were where you could see who a person really was at that moment. Those were the shots that Angela kept as her true favorites. As she moved through the crowd, she took many photos, thoroughly enjoying herself until Jane and the sparkle girls arrived. And of course, even with a room full of people to feed off, Jane couldn't resist a target like Angela.

"See, girls?" said Jane, loud enough for everyone to hear. "This is what I mean. With all the beautiful people to be focusing on, there you stand like a loser, taking pictures of plants on a window sill."

"Jane, I am so glad you came," said Emma. "I was hoping to do a page in the yearbook called 'The Mindless Gap,' and I couldn't think of a better person to use in the center of the page."

"Very funny, Emma. Oh, and by the way, the 1950's called for you. They're looking to get their glasses back!"

Just as Emma was going to reply, Mrs. Wren came out of her classroom. Right away, Jane went to see how she could kiss up to the teacher.

"Everyone find a seat; I want to get started right away. After talking to each of you and going through the signup sheet, I have put together a list of what I would like you to be working on and the person with whom I would like you to work. I don't want you to be upset if you are not assigned the tasks you originally asked for. In those cases, I thought your talents could be better served elsewhere and I want to push you to try something different," stated Mrs. Wren.

The assignment sheet went around. Jane got it before Angela and Emma, and whispered to her look-a-likes before handing it to them. As Angela expected, she was assigned the position of photographer. What she didn't expect to see was that Emma was not. With a gasp, Emma read out loud, "Chief Editor?" Last year's chief editor had graduated, so many people had speculated about whom would get the job; no one thought it would be Emma, although Angela thought Emma would be perfect.

"Congratulations, Emma!" said Angela.

"I don't know what to say! I'm speechless. I figured I would be taking pictures with you."

"Don't worry. I'm sure there are some other people here that can point a camera. Let's see ... oh no, look!" said Angela, with a defeated look on her face.

Emma took the paper and said, "Jane? Is she kidding? Did you do something to make Mrs. Wren angry?"

"I can't imagine," replied Angela, as she struggled with her disappointment.

Mrs. Wren continued to organize the kids into groups so they could brainstorm a theme for the year book. Many suggestions were made, but the group eventually voted for 'The ties that bind'. The theme didn't win by an overwhelming majority, but choosing it gave them a start. Now that the theme was settled, the kids broke into their assigned work groups. They would stay in the same work group for the remainder of the project. Angela's group consisted of Jane; one of Jane's lackeys, named Mercedes; Ben; and Justine. Angela did not know much about Mercedes; Angela only remembered her because of her unusual name. Ben and

Justine were photographers last year and were known to be really good. Angela wasn't sure Jane knew how to use a camera.

Just as Jane was ready to take control of what they were going to do, Mrs. Wren approached the group and said, "Here are my photographers. I have great faith in all of you to produce some wonderful photos. I would like Angela to be in charge of the group. She will coordinate your assignments and make sure that you are all on the same page. Here is a list of the groups currently in the school. I will let you guys put together a shooting schedule so that you can arrange everything you need. Ms. Cray has offered her equipment and any help you may need on your photos."

Jane was not happy to hear that she was not to be the leader of the group, and her unhappiness was obvious by the look on her face. Either Mrs. Wren didn't notice, or she chose to ignore it; probably the latter. Angela saw an excellent opportunity to get Jane out of her hair. There were a few groups that contained most of Jane's friends. Angela assigned these groups to Jane and Mercedes, since she figured Jane wouldn't be touching a camera. When Jane and Mercedes moved off to another table to coordinate, Ben told her that Mercedes was in his photography class and actually had some talent. Angela was skeptical, but didn't have any reason not to trust Ben's judgment. After an hour or so, the team had a good working schedule for group shots and had some ideas about upcoming events they should cover. For the events that had already taken place, they could solicit photos from other students or teachers that might have been there. Once the photographers had accomplished all they needed to finish for the day, Angela ended the meeting and decided to work on her photography assignment. She also wanted to take some more candid shots for the yearbook staff page. When the rest of the small groups had finished up their work, Emma and Angela headed out to the late bus.

"How's your arm?" asked Emma.

"It's okay now. I actually forgot about it," replied Angela as she removed the bandage. "Look, there's not even a mark, and the scratch I got from the pricker bush in our yard is gone."

"That is weird. That must have been some aloe on that band aid to make your arm heal so fast. How was working with Jane? I can just imagine how helpful she can be!" teased Emma.

"Besides all the snide comments, she actually was helpful. She knows a lot of people in the groups we are photographing. I'm sure later when she and Mercedes start taking candids we will have more arguments, but for now there were only little sparks," returned Angela.

"What are you up to tonight? Do you want some company after dinner?" asked Emma.

"Sure, but I have some homework that I need to do first; come over when you're done eating and we can hang out," answered Angela.

Fortunately for Angela, her house was close to the school and the first stop on the late bus. After saying good bye to Emma, she headed into her empty house. Usually when Angela came home on the late bus, her mom would be home, so it was strangely quiet when she opened the door. Not really looking to get into a complicated dinner, Angela decided to hit the canned goods.

"Ah, one of my favorite chefs: Chef Boyardee," Angela said when she reached for the Beefaroni. As she grabbed the can she thought she felt a slight breeze. When she turned to look in the direction the breeze had come from, there was nothing. 'Strange,' she thought. One minute and thirty-five seconds later, dinner was ready. After her gourmet "meal in a can," it was time to hit the books. Homework was usually done in the kitchen as her mom cleaned up but today she figured since she was by herself she would use the desk in her room.

Stepping into her room, she knew right way something wasn't right. Glancing over to her desk, her heart almost stopped. There, in the center of her desk, lay the green stone that had shocked her during photography class. She was dumbfounded. How could it be here? At first she was only afraid to touch it; and then she quickly looked around, now afraid that she was not alone. All she could think of was all the kids in the news that had disappeared. Her closet was always open and packed full of stuff, so she knew no one was in there, and she reached for her tennis racquet. A weak weapon for sure, but it was that or the back scratcher. She went from room to room upstairs and checked every corner and closet. Her imagination ran wild. Every creak of a floorboard or swoosh of a curtain was someone sneaking up behind her. The wind blowing outside was someone trying to get in. Every sound put her on edge. 'Nothing so far,' she thought. She eased her way down the stairs, very nervous about what she would find. First she checked the dining room, then she went around to the kitchen. When she entered the family room, the doorbell suddenly went off! The racquet went up in the air and Angela jumped two feet off the ground, fell over the coffee table and landed on her butt.

'Emma!' she thought as she rubbed her backside. Angela went to the door and peeked out the sidelight. There, with a backpack and a sleeping bag, was Emma. The relief Angela felt poured over her like a wave at the beach.

"Thank goodness it's you," said Angela, ripping the door open.

"Hi. I figured it would be easier to just spend the night. Wait, what do you mean? Who were you expecting?" asked Emma.

"It's been a little crazy here," said Angela, and she explained everything that had just happened while locking all the doors and windows.

"I want to see this rock," said Emma, as she entered Angela's room.

"Wait! Don't touch it!" But Angela was too late. Emma picked up the rock and held it up for closer inspection. Nothing happened.

"Looks like a green rock to me. Perhaps some type of green quartz. It's pretty," said Emma as she handed the rock back to Angela.

Angela held out her hand and braced herself for the shock that she anticipated to come, but again there was nothing. The rock fell into her hand and there was no pain. It seemed a little warm, but otherwise it was just a pretty rock.

"The big question," said Angela, "is how did it get in here? I know I didn't bring it. It was here when I got here."

"And you're certain that it is the same rock?" asked Emma.

"If it isn't, it is a perfect copy," replied Angela

"Were all your doors locked?" returned Emma.

"They were when I got home, but I didn't lock the door after I came home. I don't usually. It's locked now, that's for sure."

"Well, we should check the house one more time, since someone obviously snuck in and put the rock on your desk. The rock obviously didn't get here by magic. Let's finish checking the house, and then get some ice cream. I find that many things look better when you're looking across the top of a bowl of ice cream."

"Agreed. Someone must have seen me at school with the rock, and then thought it would be funny to bring it here. But who would do that and why? It's not funny; in fact, it is a little creepy."

After checking the house one last time, the girls got two big bowls of ice cream and sat down to do the last of their homework. They didn't have too much to do, so movie time came quickly.

"Probably not the best night for a horror movie. How about 'Twilight' again?" asked Angela.

"Sounds good to me," answered Emma.

"Okay, you set up the movie and I'll pop the popcorn," said Angela, as she tossed Emma the remote. As Angela rolled off the couch, she felt something in her pocket. She reached in and pulled out the green rock.

"I don't remember putting this in my pocket," thought Angela out loud.

"What? How did that get there? I saw you put that on your desk when we left your bedroom," answered Emma.

"I thought I did, too." Angela walked over to the buffet and placed the stone in the top drawer. Emma ran upstairs to check to see if the rock was there.

"There is nothing upstairs," said Emma.

"Now we are both certain as to where it is. I am going to make the popcorn and get some soda," said Angela as Emma stared at the stone.

Twenty minutes or so into the movie, the phone rang. Angela reached over to the phone to check the caller ID. She figured it would be her mom and she was right. That happened a lot. Whenever she would think about her mom she would usually call.

"It's my mom," said Angela as she got up.

"Perfect timing. I have to pee," said Emma.

Just then, Angela absent-mindedly slipped her hand into her pocket and there was the rock. Angela's face went pale.

"What's wrong?" said Emma.

Angela held out the rock mutely, and the two of them stared at it while the answering machine answered the phone. Emma took the rock and Angela quickly answered the phone. They both looked at the buffet. Emma walked over and opened the drawer. No rock. She looked at Angela and shook her head.

Emma was too scientifically-minded and fact-based to accept what she had in her hand. She and Angela had been together the entire time since the rock was put in the drawer. She could hear Angela telling her mom that they were watching a movie and couldn't find the remote to pause it. Angela hung up the phone and joined Emma in the living room. Emma handed her the rock.

As the rock touched Angela's hand, it began to glow.

"Look at that!" exclaimed Angela. "It's glowing!"

"At this point, nothing surprises me," observed Emma as she stared into the green glow. Just then the glowing stopped.

"Okay, this night ranks as one of the weirdest I have ever seen," said Angela. "Have you ever heard of anything like this before?"

"Never," answered Emma with a blank stare. "This is new to me."

"I'm not sure what to think. This type of thing doesn't happen in real life. I have a rock that, after first zapping me, now follows me around. If that is not enough, it now glows when I touch it. And now my arm hurts again!" Angela said while collapsing onto the couch.

"I want to test it again. Let me see it," said Emma.

Angela handed her the rock and Emma walked to the front door, opened it, and threw the rock as hard as she could out the front door.

"Let's see if it comes back from that," said Emma. "I think I am ready to end this night and go to bed."

"Me, too," said Angela, "I will get you some towels."

Angela and Emma turned out the lights and went upstairs. Sitting on the top step was the rock.

"Looks like you got a pet rock," said Emma, staring at it.

"Yeah, and it already knows some tricks." Angela reached down and picked it up. The stone glowed in her hand. "Now, the question is, what do I do with it?"

Angela set the stone on her desk and Emma unrolled her sleeping bag on the floor. Usually Emma slept in the guest room or sometimes they both fell asleep in the family room, but tonight neither of them wanted to be alone. After Emma fell asleep, Angela got out of bed, picked up the stone and moved to the window in the dormer. She stepped on her chair and crawled out onto the roof. After getting all the way out, she swung her legs around and leaned against the outside of the window. Angela loved being out at night, and she really loved being this high. She had spent many nights out here looking up at the stars. Even with all the stories about kids disappearing, she still did not want to stay inside. Tonight, though, she decided that she would stay where she was. She didn't want Emma to wake up and freak out if Angela were gone.

When Angela's father died, she took it really hard. She didn't really want to talk to anyone. Many people tried to talk to her and some even had good advice, but nothing really helped. Angela needed to find a way to deal with her grief on her own. For a year, she was pretty depressed. Her mom was very supportive and gave Angela all the space she needed. Her mom tried to get Angela to talk, and some nights Angela would open up a little, but it wasn't until they moved here and Angela started her new night-time rituals that she really started to accept the fact that her father was gone and that it was no one's fault. He didn't want to leave them, but he had no more choice in the matter than Angela or her mom did. When Angela was out at night, the sense of abandonment would be less and, eventually, that feeling of loss was something she could live with. Soon, she started feeling better into the day time. Finally, she came to grips with the fact that her dad was gone. One day, when it was her time, she hoped to see him again. From that point on, she continued her night time wanderings but she never returned to the person she was before her father was gone. Her mom knew she sat out on the roof and even if her own fear of heights prevented her from understanding why Angela would sit out there, she was happy that Angela was finally moving on. She didn't know about the walks Angela took in the woods. Angela figured that was best.

Now, there was this stone. As Angela thought about the stone and the rest of her day, something else continued to bother her and she just couldn't put a finger on what it was. Something she had seen today didn't sit right with her, but she just couldn't remember what it was or why it bothered her. At that moment, something flew between her and the moon and a huge shadow passed over her. By the time Angela looked up, whatever had caused the shadow was gone, but she knew by the size of the shadow that the flying object must have been really big. When she looked down into her hand, she saw her rock glowing again. 'What am I going to do with you?' thought Angela.

As she turned to head back inside, her arm began to tingle again. She thought that she was over this by now. As she crawled through the window, the tingle turned into pain and shot up through her arm. The pain became unbearable and started to move through her entire body. She barely made it back into the room when the pain brought her to her knees. She grabbed the side of her bed, gasping, and pulled herself in. When the pain reached her head, her vision blurred until she finally blacked out. As Angela curled into a ball, racked with pain, the stone glowed bright green. Angela regained consciousness just long enough to see a large black shape come into her window and move across the floor. Before the green glow from the rock became bright enough to see what was coming towards her, the pain redoubled and Angela once again succumbed to the blackness.

3

ANGELA 2.0

Angela awoke to the beeping of her alarm ... both of them, actually. Her mother had taken the liberty of adding her own alarm to Angela's room while she was away. Angela suspected that a phone call would be on its way as well, to help with the wake-up process. Sure enough, two seconds later, the phone rang. Angela sprang up to answer it. Then she paused. She noticed that she had just sprung out of bed. Angela did not spring, she never sprang, and especially not out of bed first thing in the morning at 6:00 am! She regained her senses and answered the phone. Her mom was just as surprised as Angela was to hear her daughter answer on the third ring.

"Morning, Mom."

"Good morning, Angela. What are you doing up? You went to bed last night, right?! You're not just going to bed now, are you?!"

"No, Mom, Emma is here, remember? She would never let us stay up all night," answered Angela.

"That's true," returned her mom. "Well, check your temperature; you must have a fever to be up this early and actually coherent."

"Thanks, Mom. Gotta go; have to get ready for school."

"Goodbye, Angela. I will call you later."

Just then, Emma sat up and leaned against the bed.

"What are you doing up? What time did you go to sleep? I expected to have to drag you out of bed... and my goodness, Angela," exclaimed Emma, "since when do you look this good in the morning!?"

"What do you mean?" returned Angela, as she looked into the mirror over her dresser. At first she didn't really notice anything, but with a second glance she saw what Emma was talking about. The zit she had been fighting seemed to have given up and retreated back to where it came from, and there were no dark circles under her eyes for a change. Her hair looked like she had just come from the hair dresser, and her normally pale complexion seemed to have gotten a tan. She did look good.

"What time did you go to bed?" asked Emma again.

"That's a good question," said Angela. Then, some of the evening came back to her in a rush. "I was sitting on the roof..." Normally that statement would take people off guard, but Emma was not new here. "...the rock started to glow again and ... and I'm not sure. I kinda remember something like a shadow flying in front of the moon, but I can't remember much of anything else. The memory seems to be right there but I just can't remember. I must have gone to bed late, though. I do remember sitting on the roof for a while."

"Anyway," said Emma, "I have never seen you so alert and awake before ten in the morning!"

"Very funny, but I have to admit I feel really good. My arm doesn't hurt at all. I think it is okay now," observed Angela as she flexed her hand.

"Well, we all don't look that good first thing in the morning. I have to go to the bathroom and get ready," groaned Emma, as she picked herself off the floor. "I am not meant to sleep on the floor anymore." Emma stretched and rubbed her back, as she headed to the bathroom.

Angela laughed. That was something else she never did in the morning. 'Well, the least I can do is roll up her sleeping bag,' thought Angela. As she bent down to grab the sleeping bag, she saw something on the floor. "What's that?" said Angela, thinking out loud.

It was a feather; a big feather, as black as night, and very shiny. 'How did this get here?' wondered Angela. She set it down on the night table, rolled up the sleeping bag and got dressed. Sitting next to the feather was the rock. It was glowing green again.

Looking back into the mirror, Angela thought that Emma was right; she looked pretty good this morning. She didn't even need to do her hair. It looked better than it did all day yesterday. She looked as if she had been in the sun all day. If she didn't know better, she would even say she felt a little taller. She knew that couldn't be, but it sure felt that way.

Emma returned dressed and ready for school soon after.

"Look what I found on the floor," said Angela.

"A feather! That's pretty big. Where did it come from?" asked Emma.

"I don't know, but it seems unlikely that the wind would blow it in the window. Maybe my mom had it here for some reason and dropped it."

"I see. And your mom carries around giant feathers a lot?" asked Emma with a grin.

"Okay. I have no idea how it got here. For just a few minutes, let's pretend that nothing weird is happening and get some breakfast."

Usually a piece of toast or a bowl of cereal was all Angela could get down in the morning, but today was different. Angela was starving and eating everything she could find.

"Wow, Angela, when you get to the white part, stop eating! That's the plate! Did you forget to eat last week?" asked Emma.

"I don't know what it is, but I'm starving this morning."

Angela had made bacon, eggs, pancakes and hash browns. After her fifth egg and her third pancake, she finally started to feel full.

"I can't seem to take my mind off the kids that have disappeared. It is really bothering me. I know my mom would freak if it were me, so I can just imagine what their families are going through right now," said Angela.

"I know. I was thinking about that, too. I noticed that if you look at the towns that have reported someone lost, they form a straight line to here. What if the next kid who disappears is someone we know from Gap? "

"The last one is just so confusing. He disappeared from a room in a crowded school that had only one way out, and had a video camera. How can that even be?" asked Angela.

"I don't know; I just can't wrap my mind around it. Although it is a good distraction from your crazy rock. Where is it now?" asked Emma.

"I wasn't in the mood for any weirdness today. I decided not to fight it and stuck it in my pocket," answered Angela.

The two girls cleaned up the dishes and grabbed their bags for school. It was very pleasant not to have to actually run to make it to the bus stop. Angela felt weird today; not in a bad way, just different than she had ever felt before. She still couldn't remember going to bed last night and she kept getting flashes of a crazy dream. Just when she felt it would come to her, the dream would drop back out of reach.

"I think I can hear the bus," said Angela.

"You're crazy. I don't hear anything," said Emma.

"Really? I'm sure I can hear it," replied Angela.

Just then Emma said, "I can hear it now, barely."

A few seconds later, the bus came around the corner and stopped in front of them. The two girls shuffled into the usual bus ride mayhem. This was not usually Emma's bus, so she stopped to talk with the bus driver and give the driver the note from her mom. Angela had started for her seat when the familiar yell of "Fire!" filled her ears, immediately followed by a hail of spit balls from the back of the bus. Many of the spit balls fell short, but a few were on the mark. As Angela looked up, she could see the balls of paper in the air and, even stranger, she could see the minuscule folds of each paper and the trailing droplets of spit behind each one. As she watched them, everything slowed to give the impression that they were moving in extreme slow motion! With what seemed like a lazy effort, she grabbed a folder from the seat she was next to and easily swatted each projectile away as though they were standing still. It was done so quickly that no one really noticed except Emma, who had just finished talking to the bus driver. Now Angela was stunned. She quickly moved to her seat and sat down next to Natalie. Emma sat in the empty seat across from her so they could all talk together. Emma stared at Angela and noticed the slight shake of her head. Angela was not ready to talk about this in front of Natalie.

"Did you guys go for a makeover without me?!" admonished Natalie.

"No. Why would you ask that?" said Angela, totally confused.

"What do you mean? Look at you. You have never looked this good since I met you!" said Natalie, obviously feeling slighted.

"Trust me; we didn't do anything last night but watch a movie. I noticed, too. Angela is just having a good hair day," said Emma.

"It's not just her hair; it's her skin, her color, even her nails. Look at them! What did you do? You've got to tell me!" cried Natalie. "Are you kidding me? You even look taller!"

"Okay, you guys, I'm starting to feel a little self-conscious. I have done nothing different this morning; I didn't even comb my hair! Let's talk about anything other than me right now."

"You didn't even comb your hair!!! That is how you woke up?!" said Natalie. People were starting to turn and stare. Even when Natalie was not being loud intentionally, her voice tended to carry. Angela's new complexion was now turning a proper shade of red.

"I have to get up at 5:30 to shower, do my hair, makeup and clothes, and if I'm lucky I can eat something before I have to run to the bus. If you don't tell me your secret, I am never going to speak to you again!"

"We should all be that lucky. Now hush, Natalie!" scolded Emma. "I was with her the entire time and she did nothing that I didn't do! Angela is having a good hair day and that's all. You need to stop being so superficial!"

That did it. Natalie huffed and turned to look out the window. Angela's red face was now fading back to its new healthy glow and she thanked Emma with her eyes. To her relief, the rest of the bus trip went on in relative silence.

Unfortunately, the same could not be said when she got off the bus. As she walked to homeroom, people who never gave her the time of day stopped what they were doing to look at her. Some of the boys who never gave her a second glance were actually saying hi to her. She never really cared about that before, but she had to admit it was flattering. She had almost made it to homeroom when the familiar, "Hey, loser!" rang through the hall. It was Jane. Angela didn't want to turn around, but it didn't matter. She could hear Jane coming. What was strange is she could *really* hear Jane coming. Without turning around, she knew exactly who was behind her: Jane and three of her sparkle girls. She could hear what type of shoes each girl was wearing, and just by the sounds that each girl was making, she could tell exactly who they were. The changes were getting to be too much to ignore, and she was a little scared about what was happening to her.

Before Angela could turn, Jane began, "As much as I hate it, I was told by Mrs. Wren that I had to submit all my photos through..." and as Angela turned, Jane stopped talking in mid-sentence.

"What?" Jane seemed a little taken aback. "Really? Do you think a little makeup and a brush is going to make a difference? You're still just a loser," said Jane.

"It's good to see you, too, Jane. Is there something you wanted to say or should we just consider ourselves lucky to be in your presence?" asked Emma.

"Ugh. Mrs. Wren told me that all our pictures need to go through Angela. I can't imagine why, but she wouldn't budge, so here."

Jane handed Angela an envelope full of pictures.

"Did you take these, or did Mercedes take them?" asked Angela.

"These are mine. Mercedes' photos are with Ms. Cray. They are printing out now," answered Jane.

"Wow, Jane, looks like you had the camera pointing in the right direction on every single one of these," smiled Angela.

"Whatever." With that, Jane walked away.

Angela and Emma looked through the pictures and realized that Jane really could take a good picture.

"Who would have thought," said Emma, as she left Angela for homeroom.

Just as Angela walked into her homeroom, she began to feel dizzy. Staggering to her desk, she found that she was being bombarded with a multitude of sounds that she had never really heard before. Quiet conversations were booming in her ears. One kid in the back of the room sneezed and she almost fell over. Laughing, talking, yelling... all the sounds of the room were coming at her at once and she was almost ready to scream. Then she heard something new: a thumping sound. She tried to focus on that one sound and realized it was the sound of her own heart. She gave all of her attention to this sound and gradually the other sounds faded. Keeping focused on the sound of her heart, she began to slowly introduce other sounds into her consciousness. First, the heavy breathing of someone two rows back. As she focused on the breathing, she could tell without looking where the person was sitting. She closed her eyes and slowly brought each of the other sounds in. She focused on one at a time, easing them all in until the sounds no longer beat on her ear drums. She opened her eyes expecting everyone to be looking at her, but no one was. Soon after, the noise returned to its normal volume and the announcements came over the loud speaker.

After the bell rang, everyone filed out to head to first period. This meant history for Angela. Unlike every other day, Angela did not feel tired at all. Not only was she able to pay attention during class, she was actually able to participate. Her teacher was amazed when her hand went up to answer a question about the war of 1812. English and geometry also went very well.

What surprised her most was gym. Dodge ball week continued, and when the teams were chosen, Angela was again picked last. She definitely received many second looks today when she came out of the locker room, but apparently no one thought the new look would help her throwing arm. All the kids lined up on each side of the gym as their teacher lined up all the balls in the middle of the gym. When they were all ready, the whistle blew and the class went into a sprint. Angela reached the center of the room, grabbed two balls and threw them before the other team had even crossed halfway to the center. Two very shocked boys were hit in the chest so hard they had no time to catch the balls. As a matter of fact, they were both too winded to do anything but focus on trying to breathe again! Angela picked up two more balls and ran back to her side of the gym. She spotted Mark Peters across the gym. He had taken great pleasure in hitting her yesterday several times. With more strength than she thought she had, she threw the ball hard; not at where he was, but where she knew he was headed. He ran right into the throw and caught it in the face, which knocked him hard to the ground. Angela was amazed; almost as amazed as Mark was. As she was watching Mark pick himself up, she heard something cutting through the air. The ball was coming at her from the side. Without looking, she brought up the ball in her hand and deflected the incoming projectile without a glance. Swinging a full 360 degrees, she launched her ball in the exact direction from which the ball had come at her. Hearing a satisfying thump, she knew the ball had hit its mark. Five minutes later, the round was over. Only three people on her team got hit before Angela had finished off the other side. When all the balls had hit the ground, everyone was staring at her. Angela realized that she was having so much fun that she hadn't really thought about how all this was starting to look. At the beginning of the next round, Angela pretended to hurt her ankle and sat out the rest of the class. Angela had hoped that everyone would forget what happened by the time the bell rang, and for the most part she was right. Angela quickly left the locker room to head for lunch. She needed to talk to Emma.

As she walked into the lunch room, many heads turned to look at her. Earlier, Angela had liked the attention, but now she wanted to put her head in a bag. She moved to the table as quickly as possible and collapsed in a chair. Emma sat down soon after.

"Hey, Angela, dodge ball again today?" asked Emma.

"Yes, but..." started Angela but Emma cut in before she could finish.

"I know. An hour of people throwing things at you."

"Actually, it was different this time. I really need to tell you..." Again, Angela tried to speak, but Natalie came to the table and collapsed into a chair. Angela liked Natalie, but

Natalie wasn't great at keeping secrets so Angela had to stay quiet.

"Hey, Emma, hey, Wonder Woman!" said Natalie as she smiled at Angela.

"What do you mean?" asked Angela

"Pete met me at my locker and told me about your gym class," answered Natalie.

"What's that about me? You guys talking about me again? If I had a nickel for every girl that talked about ..." said Pete as he sat down.

Natalie cut him off, saying, "You would OWE about 50 bucks. Now keep quiet while I'm talking."

Pete ignored her and said, "Hey, Angela... oh, my! Ow!!!"

Natalie saw Pete's eyes pop out of his head as he saw Angela and elbowed him in the ribs, saying, "It's a good hair day and that's all, Pete! Anyway, Pete told me that you were a wild woman in dodge ball today; throwing, catching, dodging? What gives? I had gym with you last year and it was not pretty! First the new look and now this? "

"It was just a fluke; really, I am just having a good day, that's all."

"I know, right? It must be some good day. Anyway, did you see what that Brie girl was wearing?"

Natalie continued to speak and Angela and Emma just looked at each other. Emma looked worried and Angela didn't know what to make of anything that was happening. What she did know was that Natalie was in full stride and not going to stop talking anytime soon. She would have to wait to talk to Emma. In the meantime, she needed to nod and say something to let Natalie think she was listening.

Finally the bell rang, and Angela and Emma set off for Photography. The girls would be able to speak freely in there, if not privately; Ms. Cray was not one for a quiet class. The two decided to choose a table toward the back of the room. No one usually sat there and it would give them a little more privacy than sitting towards the front.

"So exactly what happened in gym today?" asked Emma as they got out their equipment.

"Actually it wasn't just gym; I need to tell you about homeroom first." Angela told Emma how her ears had freaked out and what she had to do to make it go away. Then she told her all about gym class.

"Let's look at all the events over the last two days," said Emma. "First, you find this green rock that gave you a shock when you touched it. Then, it follows you home from school after disappearing from the window sill. You have a strange night that you really can't remember and you wake up looking better than I have ever seen you. Your senses start going crazy and then you become this super dodge ball player. Whatever you have going on, it is definitely not normal."

The two of them walked to the window sill to get the items they wanted to photograph. "It may seem better now, but homeroom was not an improvement. That was scary. I didn't think it was going to stop. I almost threw up my breakfast," said Angela with a grimace.

"That would have been quite the mess after all you ate this morning!" Emma laughed.

"You're not kidding," agreed Angela.

"The rock must have something to do with it. That seemed to start this whole thing off. Let me see your hand again," said Emma.

Angela held out her hand and accidentally slid her fingernail across the back of Emma's hand.

"Ow," exclaimed Emma as she drew her hand away. "Look at that!"

Emma held out her hand and showed Angela a deep scratch.

"Your nails are sharp!" complained Emma.

"That is strange." Angela ran her finger over her nail carefully and nothing happened. "Nothing," she said, as she held up her finger.

"Weird. I'm going to get a Band-aid. I'll be right back." Emma went to the back of the room to the first aid kit while Angela collected the items the two of them had picked out and went back to their table.

Emma came back and said, "Now, carefully, show me your palm." Angela did as she was told and held out her palm again. "There doesn't seem to be anything wrong with it now. I don't know what is going on, but you may have to go to a doctor. This is beyond anything I have heard of and you may need professional help."

"Forget it. No doctors; at least not until my mom gets home. She would flip if I needed to go to the doctor while she was away. Let's just see if this thing works its way out on its own, at least for now," said Angela.

"Okay, but I'm not sure where to go from here," answered Emma.

The two lapsed into silence as Ms. Cray started to wander through the room.

"What are you girls doing back here?" asked Ms. Cray.

"The lighting back here had more of what we were looking for," said Angela, who wasn't completely lying. The sun did cut through the windows and hit these tables in a way that led to better shadows.

"I see. Well, sun or no, I can tell when two people want some 'girl' time. I will leave you to it," she said with a smile. "Oh, Angela, your mom is out of town, right?"

"Yes, she is, until Friday. How did you...let me guess. She called you, too."

"Of course. Would you like to take a break from Beefaroni for one night and come over for dinner?" asked Ms. Cray.

"Did my mom put you up to this?" asked Angela.

"Maybe," said Ms. Cray, laughing.

"I think she called everyone in this town to look out for me!" exhaled Angela.

"She is just concerned for you. Any other mom would be the same way. Anyway, I will see you tonight at 6:00," Ms. Cray said with a smile as she walked away.

"It's amazing that my mom can be a thousand miles away and still embarrass me as though she was in the other room," sighed Angela.

"At least your mom didn't come to the freshman dance!" said Emma.

"I remember that, the way your mom danced to that one song...you're right. You win," laughed Angela. "Anyway, I guess we will just ride this thing out and hope it passes."

"Well, in case it does ..." Emma lifted up her camera and took a picture of Angela. "You will have a souvenir."

As the flash went off, Angela's vision went blurry. It passed quickly, but it was disorienting for a second.

"Nice," said Angela. "Let's take some pictures. I need to get my mind off this for a while."

The two of them took the shots they needed throughout the rest of the class. When the bell rang, they packed up their stuff, and after Ms. Cray said goodbye, they headed to health class. Angela was still not used to the looks she was getting from the boys and the glares she was getting from the girls. Angela started to pick up the pace; she just wanted to get out of the hallway. As they passed by the common area where the yearbook committee met, Angela thought she saw something out of the corner of her eye again. Looking around, she still didn't see anything out of the ordinary.

'That was strange,' she thought, 'but then again, what hasn't been lately?' and with that they went to Mr. Whipple's health class.

Angela and Emma shuffled in with the rest of the students and headed for their seats. Mr. Whipple was hanging some new safety posters on the walls when he noticed Angela.

"How are you feeling today?" asked Mr. Whipple.

"I feel much better, thanks," said Angela, as she held out her palm.

"You're a fast healer. Your palm doesn't seem to have a scratch on it," Mr. Whipple said as he looked at her hand. He didn't see anything on her palm, not even a scar. He had seen a lot of wounds and none of them healed in one day. "Well, I'm glad you're feeling better. And the tingly feeling is gone?"

"All gone," said Angela with a smile.

Mr. Whipple smiled in return and went to the front of the room to continue with his lesson, wondering about Angela.

After health class, Angela and Emma went to study hall knowing they would meet in the library. When Angela got there, she could tell by the look on Emma's face that Emma needed to talk. They quickly moved to the back of the library so they could be alone.

"What's going on?" asked Angela.

"Another kid disappeared this morning."

"What?! How do you know?" asked Angela, shocked.

"You know that guy Ben, the photographer for the yearbook? He is in my study hall and I overheard him saying that he came in late today and that he had seen it on the news this morning. I didn't get any details on what happened, but I heard that the kid lived close to here. He didn't go to our school, but he did live in this county."

"I can't believe it. Did you hear any details as far as where he disappeared from?" asked Angela.

"No, just that it was near here," replied Emma. "Let's check the web."

It turned out that the boy had been taken from very close by but no other details had been released as of yet.

"I need to check something else out." Angela called up a map of Pennsylvania from the Internet and pasted it into the painting program on the computer. The two of them then mapped out the locations of all the kids that had disappeared.

"Look at this," said Angela, "almost a straight line to Gap. I bet you the kid that just disappeared lived somewhere between here and this dot."

"There is no other town along this line except for Gap. I don't have a good feeling about this at all," said Emma.

"I don't either," answered Angela.

4

MS. CRAY

The girls went back to their table and tried to get some work done, but Angela had a hard time focusing. The disappearances really bothered her; more than she thought they should. She felt bad for the kids and the families who were left behind, but there was something more to it, something that she couldn't explain. It was almost like the dread that she felt before a big test that she wasn't ready for, deep in the pit of her stomach.

The bus ride home that day was, thankfully, uneventful. She was not bombarded with spit balls, and people even moved a little as she walked down the aisle. She was still getting funny looks from people, but she didn't care anymore. She was ready for this day to be over.

After letting herself into the house, she was careful to lock the door behind her. Before she could be comfortable she had to check all the rooms. When Angela was confident that she was alone, she called her mom and told her all about her day, leaving out the details of her recent improvements. She wasn't ready to tell her mom about those yet.

When Angela had finished talking on the phone, she had just enough time to finish up her homework before leaving for Ms. Cray's house. As she sat at her kitchen table, she had the strangest feeling of being watched. She looked quickly at her kitchen window and could have sworn she saw a shadow move outside. She jumped up to look out the window, but the yard was completely empty. 'I'm just jumpy because of all those kids disappearing,' she thought. Checking the time, she figured it was time to go to Ms. Cray's, welcoming the distraction she was sure her visit would bring.

Locking up behind herself, she set off for Ms. Cray's, not being able to shake that feeling of being watched. The walk was no more than ten minutes long, and she was happy that none of her overdrive senses were kicking in. For a second she could almost pretend that everything was the same as it had been a few days ago. That only lasted until the stone that wouldn't leave her side started glowing green in her pocket.

Ms. Cray's house was, well, put politely, unusual. The small front yard had many flower beds and was full of lawn ornaments, and was very heavy on the garden gnomes. The gnomes were doing all sorts of things: fishing, playing catch, and sweeping -- almost everything you could think a gnome could do. There were a few flamingos, as well as fountains and statues of various creatures. Every single item had been placed with the utmost care, and each was very clean and well kept. The small front yard was split in half by a straight cement walkway that led to several stairs leading to the front porch. The porch of the small two story home went across the entire front of the house, with a railing all the way around. The house was the only one on the street painted yellow, and although it was a little bright, it still looked nice and cheerful. The front porch did not have any lawn ornaments, but along the railings were many little trinkets and bobbles, all of which seemed to sparkle in the sun. The house was at the end of a cul-de-sac and had thick bushes and trees in front of a high wooden fence that blocked any view from the front yard into the back. There were also two rocking chairs on the porch, the only decor that actually seemed too normal to be there. Sitting on one of the chairs, sipping lemonade, was Ms. Cray.

"What do you think of my new gnome collection?" asked Ms. Cray.

"Well," answered Angela, trying not to be rude, "they are different. I don't remember them from last time I was here."

"Nope, just got them. And different is what I was going for!"

"You certainly got it." Angela shivered.

"Are you cold? Let's go inside."

Even with all the new garden gnomes, the outside did not hold a candle to the inside of the house. The neighborhood they lived in was on the older side. Each of the houses in the neighborhood, including Ms. Cray's, was one of three models. If you had been in each of those three, then you basically knew what every house looked like on the inside. Some might be reversed so the rooms were on the opposite side as in the similar models, but they were all basically the same, with one exception: Ms. Cray's house was completely different on the inside. The front door opened to one big great room with two-story cathedral ceilings that took up the entire front of the house. There were no interior walls, so you could see to the back of the house that held the open kitchen and family room area. The second floor was over the back of the house and had an open office and hallway with doors that led to three bedrooms.

The level of income in this area was not very high, which was why Angela and her mom could afford to live here, but this house had been decorated by someone who seemed to have a lot of money. Everything looked brand new and very modern. The house was immaculate, with furniture that looked very old and brand new at the same time. Along the walls were many glass display cases full of figurines that were glass, gold and silver, decorated with all types of gems. These were not like the doodads that Ms. Cray had in her classroom. These items looked very valuable.

"Go ahead, look around," said Ms. Cray. "I have added some things since the last time you were here."

So Angela did. The display cabinets just kept going and going. The front of the house held cabinets that contained all collectables, all with names that Angela didn't recognize. The cabinets towards the back of the house all held jewelry. Each one focused on a certain gem, from rubies to sapphires. Then she got to the cabinet full of diamond jewelry. Some of the diamonds were as big as marbles. Angela had no idea of the value of everything she saw, but she knew from the few times she had gone to the jewelry store in the mall that there were thousands of dollars' worth of precious stones just in this one cabinet alone.

"Ms. Cray, this place amazes me every time I see it. Your collections are fantastic!"

Ms. Cray's smile grew even wider. "You like it?!"

"I do, very much!" said Angela.

Angela remembered the first time she had ever visited Ms. Cray. She had spent hours looking at all the things that Ms. Cray had collected. She couldn't help but ask how well teachers got paid in their district, and Ms. Cray laughed. She explained that she had inherited a small fortune from her parents, but her funds seemed to be limitless.

"Go ahead and explore some more. I am almost ready with dinner." Angela looked around. She noticed the spiral stairs leading up. She had never gone up there before and didn't feel right doing so now. She wandered around the rest of the house and noticed everything she could. When she was done, her eyes drifted to the walls and there were some of the most beautiful photographs that she had ever seen. Many of them were signed, and she recognized the names of some very famous photographers. The floor was hardwood, but covered with many area rugs that looked so soft and clean that she was afraid to walk on them. She took her shoes off and put them to the side, just to be safe. The large sectional sofa faced a huge flat screen TV over a fireplace with a beautifully ornate antique-looking mantle. Angela sat down on the couch.

"You can turn on the TV if you want," said Ms. Cray from the kitchen. Angela looked down at the coffee table in front of the couch. It had four large remotes on it. Angela was pretty good with this sort of thing, but she was still hesitant to pick one up and push a button.

"That's okay," said Angela, "I am still just taking everything in. There is just so much to see."

Ms. Cray smiled again, "You're too sweet. Come sit down, it's time to eat." Angela went over to the island and climbed onto one of the tall bar stools. Ms. Cray set a plate in front of her holding what looked to Angela like a gourmet meal. The ceramic plate held fish stuffed with crab meat and a side of crisp asparagus, as well as a twice-baked potato.

"This looks amazing!" exclaimed Angela. "You can cook, too?!"

"What? This? I just threw this together," answered Ms. Cray with a slight blush on her cheeks.

"That's funny, when I 'just throw something together' it involves a can opener and 'O' shaped pasta!" said Angela.

"Spaghetti-O's? My goodness, Angela, you can do better than that!" admonished Ms. Cray with a grin.

The two started to eat while they talked about photography. Angela wanted to tell Ms. Cray about all the changes she was going through, but she didn't know if it all sounded too crazy. It also seemed as though Ms. Cray was avoiding any topic that would easily let Angela bring up her new abilities. Angela decided that she wasn't ready to tell anyone other than Emma just yet.

Soon after they were done with dinner, Ms. Cray brought out a tray of brownies from the oven. Ms. Cray knew how much Angela loved brownies. Finally, Angela yawned and looked at her watch. "Wow, it's 11:00. I better get going." Just then, a very cold breeze came through the open window, as cold as it had been earlier in the day. For a second, Angela thought that Ms. Cray looked nervous, but she regained her composure so quickly that Angela thought it might only have been a trick of the light.

"It is pretty late. Why don't you just spend the night here? I have a spare room and it is always ready for a guest." Angela was about to protest, but then Ms. Cray said, "Really, Angela, you can spend the night here." The words seemed to echo in Angela's ears and every objection she had seemed not to matter.

"Okay, that sounds good," replied Angela, "Is it okay if I use your phone? It looks like the battery on my cell phone died, and I want to let my mom know where I am in case she tries to call."

After Angela got off the phone, she and Ms. Cray went up the stairs to the second floor. Ms. Cray showed her the bathroom and the room she would be sleeping in. The decor upstairs was as lavish as it was downstairs. The bedroom Angela would be using had a large four-poster bed and was decorated all in blue. It was very pretty. There was a vase with flowers on the dresser, as if Ms. Cray had expected her to spend the night from the beginning.

"I will get you some pajamas to wear tonight, and in the morning we can stop at your house so you can get fresh clothes on the way to school."

After saying goodnight, Ms. Cray went into her room and closed the door. When Angela was done in the bathroom, she walked back down the hallway. She looked up at the first door and saw that it looked very different from the other doors in the hallway, and even though she didn't want to intrude, she tried to open it. It was locked, really locked. The door knob didn't even wiggle. She thought that was strange. The next door opened easily to her room. The bed was so soft and comfortable that she didn't want to fall asleep and miss any of it. Before Angela could think about anything else, she was fast asleep.

Angela woke in the middle of the night. The stone on her night stand was glowing bright in the darkness.

"Are you kidding me? What time is it?" mumbled Angela as she sat up in bed. She looked over at the clock on the nightstand; it was 2:00 am. She loved the spicy food she had had for dinner but it always made her thirsty. She got out of bed and went out to the hallway, intending to head down to the kitchen for something to drink. When she looked over the railing down into the great room, several of the lighted jewelry cabinets were glowing. The sight was breathtaking: all the crystal and precious stones were casting reflections throughout the house, as if she were in a glimmering cave with rubies and diamonds everywhere. As she passed by Ms. Cray's room, she heard voices.

'Who could she be talking to at this hour?' thought Angela. She put her ear to the door and tried to hear some of the conversation. Normally, she would never have done this but things were too strange right now to ignore anything that might help her figure out what was happening.

"She is asleep right now. No, I don't think it is time, it's too early. Yes, I know how important this is but there is so much responsibility and... I know, but I was not so young and already on my own. Yes, and also very stubborn, and that is why I am not going to change my mind. I will see you tomorrow."

Angela moved away from the door, and went down the stairs. 'Who was she talking to? It couldn't be about me, but if not, who?' Angela was too tired to piece this together right now. She just needed a drink of water. The reflected light throughout the room made it very easy to move around in the dark. Everything in the cases seemed to look very different in the strange lights. She wandered through the great room and over to the kitchen. As she approached the counter she saw a shimmer on the floor. She bent down to pick it up and saw that it was another feather, just like the one she had found in her bedroom.

'Where are these things coming from?' At that moment Angela spun around to the window. She could feel that someone was watching her. This time she saw it: a face in the window. She couldn't make out the features of the face in the split second she saw it but someone was definitely looking at her from the outside. As she turned to run upstairs, she almost ran into Ms. Cray, who was standing right behind her! Angela had never even heard her coming, even with her improved hearing.

"Angela, what's wrong?" asked Ms. Cray.

"There was someone at the window!" yelled Angela.

Ms. Cray looked to the window and ran for the back door as she yelled over her shoulder, "Lock the door behind me and stay in the house until I get back."

Angela wanted to protest, but there wasn't time. Before she could say a word, Ms. Cray was out the door, slamming it behind her. Angela went to the window in the door but couldn't see anyone. She locked the door as she had been told and started to pace back and forth. There was a clock on the wall and Angela couldn't do anything but watch the hands go around. Finally she pulled herself away from the clock and got the water that had brought her down to the kitchen in the first place.

Finally, after the longest half hour in her entire life, there was a knock on the door that made Angela jump out of her skin.

"Angela, it's me," said Ms. Cray from behind the door. "Open up. Whoever was out here before is gone now."

Angela opened the door, let in her teacher and asked, "Did you see anything? Who was out there?"

"I believe that someone was there, but I didn't see anyone," answered Ms. Cray.

"What if he comes back? Shouldn't we call someone? Like the police?" Angela was now starting to unravel.

Hearing the tremor in her voice, Ms. Cray assured her, "Angela, calm down. Do you think I could have a collection like this and not have taken certain precautions to keep it all safe?" Ms. Cray then said something that made Angela take a step back. "You are going to be fine, Angela; there is nothing to worry about here." It wasn't the words that calmed Angela but there was something extra in Ms. Cray's voice that made Angela feel all warm inside. Immediately she felt safe and calm and for some reason she no longer feared what she had seen outside.

"I guess I am going to go back to bed," said Angela in a sleepy voice.

"That sounds like a good idea to me," smiled Ms. Cray. On the outside, Ms. Cray seemed very calm but inside she was worried. When Angela got back to her room, her bed seemed even more comfortable and, thankfully, she fell asleep easily again.

The next morning, Angela awoke to the smell of pancakes and bacon. She was not quite as hungry as yesterday, but she was still very hungry again. She walked down the steps and there was Ms. Cray, dressed and ready for the day. There were pancakes, eggs and bacon all heaped on a plate waiting for her. "You must be starving. Here, eat," said Ms. Cray.

Angela thought that was a strange thing to say, but she didn't argue; she was hungry. After breakfast, Angela offered to wash the dishes but Ms. Cray told her not to worry about them and to head upstairs to get dressed. When Angela got into the bathroom, she again looked as perfect as she had the morning before. Angela was starting to appreciate the convenience of it all. When she came down, Ms. Cray was also ready to go. Angela had never really looked at Ms. Cray as closely as she did now. Angela had never been into jewelry before so she hadn't noticed the jewelry that Ms. Cray wore. Now Angela saw that Ms. Cray was wearing red ruby earrings, a blue sapphire ring and a diamond bracelet and necklace. The way the jewels sparkled in the light made Angela realize that everything about Ms. Cray sparkled. She decided that she liked that about her. In the car, Angela could tell that Ms. Cray was thinking about the previous night. She was very quiet and hadn't said anything since they had left Angela's house. To break the silence, Angela asked, "Did you hear about the last disappearance yesterday?" Ms. Cray slammed on the brakes.

"There was another one? When? I didn't hear anything."

Angela stared at Ms. Cray in amazement.

"I'm sorry, I don't..." started Ms. Cray.

"It's okay. This is bothering everyone," interrupted Angela, but she hadn't expected so strong a reaction.

"I know. I'm sorry. I don't know what got into me. Angela, there is something..."

Just then, a horn blew from the car behind them and Ms. Cray stopped talking and in an uncomfortable silence began driving again. Angela was afraid to say anything more, but she wanted to know what Ms. Cray had been about to say. Unfortunately, her opportunity to speak had disappeared. Ms. Cray didn't say anything more until they got to school, and then not what Angela had expected. She pulled into her spot and looked at Angela with a big grin and said, "Time for school. I'll see you in a few hours!" And with that, she got out of the car and left Angela speechless in her seat.

'If one more strange thing happens, I think I am going to freak!!!' thought Angela. And with that she headed to homeroom, on time, for the third day in a row.

Today Angela decided just to keep her head down. She had purposely worn very baggy clothes and even pulled up the hood on her hoodie. She wanted just to fade into the background. When lunch time finally came, she sat down next to Emma.

"Where were you last night? I texted you a million times and even tried calling you, but you didn't answer at home or on your cell," asked Emma.

"I'm sorry; I spent the night at Ms. Cray's. I went over for dinner and by the time we finished talking it was really late. I didn't have my charger and I forgot to charge my phone the night before so it died soon after I got there. The battery is still dead. You should see Ms. Cray's house. It was incredible!"

Angela was able to tell Emma everything about the previous night before Natalie caught up with them. She and Pete were having a private conversation and Angela wasn't sure if they were breaking up again, or getting back together. Finally the bell rang and they headed off to photography. She knew that Ms. Cray would not be able to talk to her as she had this morning, but it still felt good to see her. Today Angela and Emma were ready to develop some pictures. They were using 35mm cameras for this last project, so they were going to need the dark room, which was a wonderful place to talk privately since there was only room for two people, and the room was shut up tight so the light would not get in. Angela started on the photos that she had taken at the first yearbook meeting. She was pleased by all of the shots and felt that any one of them would suffice for her assignment this week. There were some really good candid shots, too. As she looked at the pictures hanging up on the drying line, she kept focusing on one of the shots more than the others.

"Something is weird about this picture," said Angela.

"What do you mean?" Emma stepped over to get a better look. "It came out fine, not blurry at all," replied Emma.

"No, not the developing, it's something else, but I can't put my finger on it." She got out the negative for the shot and made another print, but this time she enlarged the print into a 5x7. She went to set the photo out to dry but there wasn't enough room on her line.

"You can put it over with mine. I have room," said Emma. After that, the two of them put away the chemicals and when enough time had passed, they were able to open the door.

"How'd it go, girls?" asked Ms. Cray with her usual happy tone.

"It went well," answered Emma. "We got some pretty good shots."

"I can't wait to see them," said Ms. Cray. They had spent most of the time in the dark room and now decided to just hang out and see what everyone else was doing for the last ten minutes of the class.

Before the bell rang, Emma went back into the dark room to get their pictures. She came out as the bell was ringing.

"I only had one folder, so I put them all together." Emma had noticed that Angela did not have her portfolio with her, so Emma put all the photos in hers.

"I forgot to grab it this morning. I was in a rush, with Ms. Cray waiting in the driveway," explained Angela.

"Don't worry. I can stop by tonight after dinner and we can go through them," said Emma.

"Okay. I will see you in the library," said Angela.

"Oh, I can't. I have an editor's meeting with Mrs. Wren," frowned Emma.

"No problem. I have tons of geometry and history homework. I'll stay in study hall today. Why don't you stop by around 6:30?"

With that, the two girls went their separate ways. They had no idea that they would not see each other again for a very long time.

5

A MIDNIGHT RUN

As Angela walked from the bus stop to her house, she could see a bag sitting on the front porch. She didn't need to get very close to read the note; actually she could read the note from all the way across the yard. It said, 'This should taste better than Spaghetti-O's.' Angela laughed; they were the leftovers from last night's dinner.

'Ms. Cray must have dropped them off after school,' thought Angela. Ms. Cray was right, though, those leftovers would taste a lot better than Spaghetti-O's! Angela was an okay cook, but she didn't seem to have the desire to really put something big together with her mom not home, so the leftovers were really appreciated.

Not forgetting the strange things that had happened over the last few days, especially since the stone was always in her pocket now, she checked the house and locked it up nice and tight. 6:30 came and went, but Emma didn't arrive. Angela thought Emma's absence was strange, but if Emma was late Angela was sure she had her reasons. When 8:00 came, Angela decided to text her. Reaching for her cell phone, she realized that it was still not charged. So, using the house phone, she called both Emma's home number and her cell, leaving messages on both since she only got voicemail. Angela took advantage of the time to relax and catch up on some of her photography magazines. She was really behind and had several months stacked up waiting for her. At around 11:00, she was startled by the phone ringing. It was her mom. After catching her up on the day's events, minus the strange guy in the window, she told her mom about dinner with Ms. Cray. Her mom was such a good listener.

"I'll have to try and get a dinner invite over there some time!" exclaimed her mom. Angela laughed and soon hung up the phone. It was now close to midnight, and Angela decided it was well past time for a midnight stroll. It had been a few days since her last walk in the woods and she felt this would be a perfect night for it. She grabbed a flash light, since there was no moon out, and went out through the back door. At the end of the back yard was the start of the game lands and acres of woods. She knew Emma and her mom would kill her if they knew she had gone out alone, but Angela lived for these times and she promised them, in her head, to make it quick.

As Angela stepped into the woods, the darkness closed around her. Her nose was assaulted with the cool damp smell of the woods, which brought back memories of all the walks she had taken in the past. This section of the forest had many mature trees whose leaves were beginning to change for the fall. Some of the vibrant colors were making an appearance and Angela reveled in it all totally taking advantage of her new enhanced sight. There was very little undergrowth in this part of the woods so Angela could wander freely among the trees. An occasional leaf would fall and Angela would focus on all the tiny veins as it hit the ground. She could even hear the leaf hit the ground, which fascinated her. Every step deeper into the forest brought new wonders to her new senses. The dry leaves crackling under her feet, the cool forest breeze moving through her hair ... . it was as if she were seeing the woods for the first time.

After ten minutes of walking, she realized that she hadn't even turned the flashlight on and she had no problems with her vision. Must be all part of Angela 2.0, she thought. She could hear every little sound as well, from the chipmunks scurrying through the leaves to insects flying through the air. Just then Angela heard something that did not belong. 'What was that?' she thought. Then she heard something else: the sound of heavy footsteps. The footsteps were not running, that much she could tell, but they were not far off, either. In addition, she could hear something cutting through the air, though the sound seemed much too large to be a bird. She was torn; she wanted to see what was soaring through the trees, but she wasn't stupid. If someone was out in the woods this late at night, it was probably not for a walk. Angela decided it was time to head back to the house. As she turned toward home, she heard a piercing screech that was so loud, she had to put her hands over her ears. Her legs gave out and she dropped to her knees. The screech filled her entire head and she felt it course through her spine. Finally the horrible noise stopped, and Angela rose shakily to her feet. She staggered a bit and then heard the sounds of fighting. She was terrified of what she might see, but she had to get a better look. There were too many strange things going on in her life just now and it was time to put a face to at least one of them!

Angela pushed deeper into the woods and then doubled back alongside the disturbance. With lightning speed, she moved into a thick bush of mountain laurel and peered back out into the clearing. At first, Angela thought she saw a huge bird, but upon closer inspection, she saw that the creature was actually a cross between a black bird and an angel. It had huge black wings on its back, and on its head were sleek black feathers that covered the back of its neck and disappeared under a leather top that wrapped between its wings and across its front. The creature was also wearing some type of leather pants, and feathers could be seen across the small of its back. Although it was hard to see, due to the speed at which they moved, the creature's arms and legs seemed to end in long sharp talons, all of which were slashing at a huge human male in the center of the clearing. Judging by the way the creature wore its clothes, as well as the grace and shape of its body, it seemed to be female. It was both beautiful and terrifying. For a time, most of Angela's attention was on the bird creature. Finally, with all her effort, she moved her focus to the man. He too was moving with blinding speed, too fast to see, almost. As he moved, Angela thought his hands were changing between clubs and claws. The bird creature stayed out of reach of those hands, but it was starting to slow down. The creature's talons were not affecting the man as Angela would have thought they might. Just then the bird looked over and saw Angela in the bush and yelled, "RUN!"

Angela got to her feet, and just before she turned to run, she saw the man's blows connect with the bird and send it through the air into a tree. Angela didn't see any more; she turned and ran as fast as she had ever moved. Before she knew it, she emerged into her yard. She sprinted to the house and through the back door. Even though she was scared out of her wits, she was exhilarated as well. Her senses were on fire and she could hear and see everything. She tried to sit down on the couch, but couldn't sit still; she paced the room and tried to relax her breathing. She replayed the night in her head and as the adrenaline started to subside, the exhilaration faded, leaving only the fear. She remembered the black feather in her room and her stomach turned. Another mad dash followed, but this time it was to the bathroom. That was the only point in the evening when she thought the Beefaroni would have made a better choice.

This whole situation had just became too real, and she needed to talk to Emma. She tried Emma's cell phone again, knowing that that call wouldn't wake Emma's parents, but again Emma didn't answer. The only thing left for Angela to do was to try to go to bed.

Sleep did not come easy. Every sound made her jump. She tossed and turned until 3:00 a.m., and finally fell asleep. At 6:00 the alarms went off and Angela crawled out of bed, feeling pretty tired. Memories of last night came back to her in a wave and her stomach turned again. What was going on? Why were all these things happening to her, and what was that bird/angel creature in the woods? She didn't get sick again, but she felt as though she might. To preoccupy her stomach, Angela got herself together and headed out to the bus stop. Natalie was on the bus but she was sitting next to Pete. He would sometimes get a ride to Natalie's bus stop so he could ride the bus with her. Angela thought that was a sweet gesture, but more importantly today, it gave her time to think. She appreciated the solitude.

Angela looked for Emma before homeroom but couldn't find her. Instead, Angela accidentally found Jane. Jane had a strange look on her face, and for the first time that Angela could remember, she was alone.

"Have you seen Emma?" asked Angela.

"Huh? Oh, no. I haven't seen her," answered Jane, somewhat distracted.

"Are you okay? Is something wrong?"

"What do you care?" snipped Jane.

"If you don't want to tell me, fine. I have my own problems," said Angela, as she turned to walk away.

"Wait. I need to tell somebody and for some reason you are the only one I think I can tell, but not here. I don't want anyone to hear." Just then the bell rang for homeroom. "You have a study hall last period, right?" asked Jane.

"I do," replied Angela.

"Okay. I will meet you in the library." And with that comment, Jane walked away.

Of all the weird things that had happened to her recently, Angela decided that this conversation with Jane was probably the weirdest.

Angela went from class to class, looking for Emma. She had a terrible feeling in her stomach and was afraid of what Emma's absence might mean.

She hurried to Mrs. Wren's English class and went right up to the teacher's desk to ask about Emma. Mrs. Wren looked up and smiled.

"Good morning, Angela, do you need something?"

"I do. I haven't seen Emma today. Did she meet with you yesterday after school?" asked Angela

"She did. And that reminds me, would you please give her this portfolio?" Mrs. Wren handed Angela Emma's portfolio case, the one she used to hold her pictures. "She left it in the common room." Angela took the case and went to her seat. She opened the case and brought out yesterday's pictures. As she paged through them, she noticed that the picture she had taken, that had struck her as strange, was in with Emma's photos. It then dawned on her that the original that had hung with her pictures was missing from her own group of photos. That was odd. Why would that one shot be missing? She looked at the photo and still had a strange feeling that something was not right. Though Angela looked at every detail of the people in the shot, she still couldn't see what was bothering her. When Mrs. Wren started the class, Angela put the photos away. 'I have to look at these again later. I know I'm missing something,' thought Angela.

Lunch could not come soon enough. Angela raced to the cafeteria to look for Emma, but she was not there. Only Natalie was in the room.

"Natalie," said Angela hurriedly, "have you seen Emma?"

"Hello to you, too," huffed Natalie. "She's not here. She must have called out sick today."

"Sick? She seemed okay last night."

"I know, right?" said Natalie in her familiar reply, "she must be faking. Probably just needed a mental health day. Hey, Pete."

"How do you know she called out sick?" asked Angela.

"I just assumed that since she is not here, she must be out sick," answered Natalie.

And with that the focus went to Pete.

'I don't get it. Why would she be home sick and not even call?' thought Angela, 'I am heading to her house right from here. I need to figure out what's going on.'

Lunch was spent mostly in silence, as Angela tried to piece this puzzle together. Soon enough the bell rang and

Angela set off for photography class. Maybe it was time to bring Ms. Cray in on her secret.

As she walked into the classroom, Angela's heart fell. Sitting behind Ms. Cray's desk was a substitute. Angela's frustration was now at an all-time high, and she was close to breaking down. She decided that she needed a distraction and reached down into Emma's photography bag to look again at her picture. She was glad she had made two prints. There was something off in this picture, and Angela wasn't going to give up until she figured it out. And finally, she did. It wasn't the people in the picture that were wrong, but something in the background of the picture. Now that she saw the oddity, she couldn't believe it had taken her so long. The picture had been taken in the commons during the first yearbook meeting, and there in the far wall was the edge of a door. The door was nothing spectacular; it was a door, just like every other door in the school. What was different about this door was that it shouldn't have been there. There had never been a door on that wall before. She was also sure that the other side of that door could not lead into any classroom. As far as she knew, there should be nothing behind that door but the girls' bathroom, and she knew that there were no other doors in there. She had a strange feeling that the answers she needed would be found behind that door.

She wanted to go there now, but she was also curious about what Jane had to say. As much as Angela wanted to sprint to the common room, she took out her camera and pretended to work until the bell rang. Finally, the class ended and she headed to the library. As she walked past the common room she glanced over, and there, as plain as day, was the door in her photo. The one thing that had been catching her eye for the last three days was standing there as if to say, 'duh, how could you miss me?!' Angela tore herself away and got to the library. The door would have to wait. She found a seat close to the door and waited for Jane to come. When Jane finally arrived, Angela got up and, without saying a word, led Jane to the back of the library to the place where she and Emma usually sat. Angela looked at Jane with a great deal of impatience.

Jane began, "I wanted to tell you earlier, because no one else will believe me and I'm not sure that you will, either, and if you do, you will probably hate me more than you already do. I came home late last night from Mark's party." Angela didn't know who Mark was, but didn't care enough to ask. "On the way home I heard someone following me. You know how it is around here. Everyone knows everyone and you don't have to worry about things like that, and the stories on the news seem so far away." At that point Jane began to cry. "Anyway, I looked back and saw this man I have never seen before. He was so tall, and no matter how hard I looked I couldn't make out what his face looked like. It was almost as if his face kept changing or something. Angela, you have to understand ... I was so scared. There is no one who will miss me. There is no one who will care when... or if ..." At this point Jane was sobbing uncontrollably. Fortunately, Ms. Boyd the librarian was busy in her office and the back of the library was empty.

"Jane, I don't understand. What are you talking about?" asked Angela.

"I screamed and started running. He ran after me and when I turned the corner to head for my house, I ran ... past ... Emma. She must have heard me scream and come out to help."

The color drained from Angela's face and she was deathly afraid of what Jane was going to say next.

"I heard Emma yell and I looked back to see her kick the man in the chest. She caught him off guard, and I thought that she would get away, but when she tried to kick him again he caught her leg and threw her so far. I saw her hit the ground hard and her phone fly out of her hand. She grabbed it and I saw her try to call someone as she crawled away. I knew she was hurt and she tried to get up but she couldn't. The man came up behind her and grabbed the back of her neck and picked her up in the air and then ... they were just ... gone."

At this point, Jane was a mess and the pain and sorrow in her eyes was apparent. Angela quickly got to her feet and Jane grabbed her arm. "Angela, I'm so sorry. It should have been me and I feel so guilty. I didn't know what to do and I tried to convince myself that it couldn't have happened, but Emma's not here, and who would believe me?"

Angela pulled away and her head started to spin. As Angela headed for the door, she realized that Emma might have been trying to call her as she crawled away from the man. Her phone was still dead; she had no idea where her charger was. Angela turned back to Jane.

"Do you have your phone charger?" she asked.

Jane nodded, and fished it out of her backpack. Angela plugged her phone into the wall and was able to turn it back on. As she looked at it, she saw that there was a message. She hesitated, brought the phone to her ear, and heard Emma's voice, "Angela, something bad is here, it was after Jane ..." was all she heard and then the sound of a struggle, and then nothing. Ignoring the protests of Ms. Boyd, who was at her desk, Angela headed for the door and went straight to the common room. As she rounded the corner, she saw the door across the way. The room was empty and no one was in the hallway. She couldn't explain her feelings, but Angela knew that she had to go through that door. With each step closer, she could feel the draw of what lay behind the door, and she didn't think she could stop even if she wanted to. She reached for the door handle, pulled, and bright light flooded the room. So bright was the light that she could not see anything in front of her. Behind her, Angela heard someone yell, "Angela, no!!!!" As she moved through the doorway, she looked back to see horror on Ms. Cray's face.

Seeing Ms. Cray's expression made Angela afraid, but it was too late. The light surrounded Angela and continued to get brighter and brighter. The light became so bright that even with her eyes closed, it was almost blinding. The stone in Angela's pocket began to burn against her leg. At that point, Angela was freed from her confusion as everything faded into darkness.

6

RAVEN

Angela started to rouse herself, but she couldn't open her eyes and her entire body hurt. Her limbs felt like lead weights, and no matter how hard she tried, she could not move. She tried to concentrate on moving just one finger, but she couldn't. Angela began to panic. All she wanted to do was to cry out, but she couldn't speak. Everything was building up inside and tears began to fall from her eyes. She screamed in her mind and could feel herself slipping away and losing everything to the darkness, but then she felt a cool hand on her forehead and a voice coming from what seemed a mile away.

"It's okay, Angela; you are going to be fine. Just sleep and it will all be better when morning comes."

'Morning?' thought Angela, pulling away from the darkness, 'What time is it? Where am I? Who is that?' So many questions rushed into her head, but before she could try to speak, one image came to her mind: Emma. Angela's single focus had been to save her friend; but before she could think of anything else, she passed out.

The next time Angela awoke, her head was pounding and it was still very hard to move, but at least she could open her eyes. She still couldn't move her head, and she felt so heavy. The fog in her head began to clear. As she looked up, she saw a thick canopy of trees, and peeking through the leaves were several stars of the night sky. The breeze moved across her face and it cooled her head, although it also made her realize how hot she felt. The sound of the insects reminded her of the woods near her home, and that helped clear her mind even more. She had hoped that she was back in her woods, but somehow she didn't think so. She tried to say something but still couldn't speak. The cool hand returned with a wet cloth, and as it was laid across her forehead, she saw that this time that hand had a face. 'Ms. Cray?' thought Angela.

"It's not time to get up yet, Angela; go back to sleep, and I promise you will feel better when you wake again. I know you have questions and I promise I will answer everything I can soon."

Now Angela was very confused. What did Ms. Cray have to do with all of this? It was all getting to be too much. Every question over the last few days flooded into her mind and started to overwhelm her. How long had she been asleep, and what was her mom going through, and what had happened to Emma? With all those worries coursing through her thoughts, she felt the tears coming once again. She tried to speak but again words failed her and tears began to fall. She was so scared she thought that she would truly die. Thankfully, the darkness found her again and she fell back into a fitful sleep.

The morning did come, and Angela awoke. She opened her eyes to see once again the canopy of trees above her. This time, the early morning sun filtered through in rays, touching the ground in several places. She could see small particles floating through the light, sparkling like tiny fireflies. It looked like she was lying in some type of grotto or clearing in the woods. Although the sun had risen, she was still cast in dark shadows from the monstrous trees surrounding the clearing. She found that she could turn her head and saw that she was lying on soft moss. A wide stream flowed through the clearing only two or three feet away. The mist from the quickly-moving water created tiny rainbows that danced across the river surface. The next thing she noticed was how warm and comfortable the air was. She was taken aback by the beauty of her surroundings.

She lay there on the moss for a moment taking in the scene, still scared to try to move. Her last memories seemed so far away, but she could still remember everything clearly. The fear suddenly came back as she remembered how she hadn't been able to move, as if her hands and legs had been bound. The crippling panic of being paralyzed forced her to stir.

Carefully, she rolled over onto her belly and propped herself up on her hands and knees. The pain that she had felt before was gone, but there was still an ache that remained in her head and all her muscles. The movement made her eyes go blurry.

'Did all that happen the night before? *Was* it the night before?' she thought.

Angela remembered going through the doorway in the common room at school, although it seemed so long ago. She sat back, looked around, and was amazed at what she saw as her vision cleared. Not far from her was a cave that burrowed into a small mound, just high enough to hold the entrance. Beyond that, on all sides, she could see that she was in a huge clearing. It almost looked like someone had carved out several football fields right in the middle of a jungle. The river snaked in and out of the woods and appeared sporadically down the left side of the field. She took a good look at the giant trees and saw that they were very different from the trees near her home. The leaves must have been two feet across and the shapes were very unusual. Thick vines wove through the trees but there was very little undergrowth, and nothing grew into the clearing. Actually, nothing but short thick grass grew in the clearing. There were sections of trees along the edges that seemed to hold back the forest from encroaching upon the space.

Angela looked over at the water and realized how thirsty she was. She leaned down to the water and looked at her reflection. In that moment, she completely forgot how thirsty she was. The face that looked back at her from the water was not the one she recognized. Angela filled her lungs to scream but what came out was far from the scream she expected. Instead it was a screech, and that surprised her almost as much. Regaining her composure, she looked back at the reflection in the stream. Her eyes were no longer brown now, but almost glowed yellow. No, not yellow, but gold, and they were huge! The lines of her face were more angular and sharp, and her hair was no longer hair but very small overlapping feathers! Even though what she saw was alien to her, she was not repulsed. Part of the fear that was welling up inside her abated just a little. She reached down to the water and again she was shocked to see that her hands had also changed. She turned them around and saw gleaming talons. They felt so strong but still very graceful and surprisingly familiar. She decided that she was going to focus on the water right now. She reached down and filled her hands with water and drank deeply. Immediately she started to feel better.

'Okay,' she thought, 'it's time to look again.' She took her focus from the water and back to the reflection. The feathers on her head went down her back and along her neck. She saw that they came around her chest and covered her entire torso down to the top of her thighs. Her pants covered her legs but she could feel where the feathers stopped and the skin continued. She staggered to her feet and looked down. Her shoes were gone and her feet had changed to include long sharp talons as well.

The drink of water had brought her to her senses. She sat for a moment and realized how dirty she was. She wasn't sure how long she had been asleep, but she felt as though it had been a while since she had a bath. She removed her clothes, steeled herself for what she was about to see and looked down. She saw that her feathers covered her like a dance leotard, traveling down her arms and around her elbows. Her skin had turned almost a caramel brown that matched her brown feathers. She reached up and felt that her ears were higher on the side of her head and completely covered by feathers. She also saw that hanging from her neck, attached to a brown leather thong, was the green stone.

"Figures you're here," she said aloud.

She slowly moved into the water and let it flow around her. She looked at her new body and although it was scary and strange, she was intrigued by the changes. She could feel a strength coursing through her that made what she had felt yesterday seem almost childlike. She sat in the water and pulled her knees up to her chest, resting her chin on her knees. She was comforted that she still had knees and almost laughed. Her hand found a hard piece of clay and she crushed it in her talons. She picked up another hunk of clay and thoughtlessly crushed that one as well. She wasn't doing it consciously, but her hand was resting near the bottom of the stream. After the third one, she noticed what she was doing and looked down. She was not crushing hard clay but rocks. She couldn't believe it. She picked up another one and turned it to rubble in her hand. Her strength was unnerving.

The water washed away the sweat from the past night and also the fog from her head. She again looked around the clearing, this time with her new senses. She saw every detail from a bug crawling on a leaf thirty feet away to the small berries on a bush across the field. As she scanned the trees lining the clearing, she heard something rustle in the leaves. Her eyes focused and she saw the creature making the stir, but she had no idea what it was. At first she thought it was a squirrel, but it had two tails and it was yellow.

'Where am I? Where did that door lead?' the thoughts blazed into her head.

Just then she heard something louder moving through the woods. This new creature made noises too loud to be those of a strange little squirrel. Angela moved out of the water and looked down at her clothes. They were pretty disgusting, and given her new feathers she decided that she didn't really need them. The noise got closer and Angela prepared herself for what might be coming. When the creature stepped into the clearing, Angela was relieved to see Ms. Cray. Forgetting how she must have looked, Angela ran to her and threw her arms around her. "Ms. Cray! I'm so glad to see you!"

"Easy, Angela," said Ms. Cray with a wheeze. "You're making it hard for me to breathe!"

"I'm sorry," said Angela as she let Ms. Cray go. "Ms. Cray…"

"Okay. Before we do anything else, you should probably stop calling me Ms. Cray. Please call me by my first name."

Angela looked confused for a moment. "What *is* your first name?

Ms. Cray said with a smile, "Raven."

"Raven, please answer my questions! What's happening to me?" asked Angela with a look of desperation. "Why am I like this? What happened to me? Where are we and how long have I been here?" and finally, with all her mental fortitude slipping away, she cried, "What happened to Emma?"

With tears in her eyes she looked down at the stone hanging around her neck and said with another sob, "And what the heck IS this thing?!"

Raven pulled Angela into a hug and said, "I know you are confused and upset. I will try to answer all your questions and I promise that I will tell you everything I can. I'll start at the beginning and tell you what I know. Come over here and sit down."

Raven lead Angela back to the area where she had woken up and the two of them sat down on the moss. "First, we are both close to home and far from home. I know that you have been experiencing some changes lately, and they were caused by this stone."

Raven pointed to the stone and continued, "When you came through that door, you were taken here, where the changes that were begun by the stone were finished."

"You mean that's when I changed into a giant bird!?" yelled Angela.

"Well, sort of. There is a bit more to it than that," answered Raven. "When there is a need, and I assure you, it does not happen often, this place searches for someone to be a type of guardian, the type of person that has the potential to handle great responsibility. When this place finds that person, it sends someone like me to prepare you. If things had gone correctly, I would have talked to you about what was going to happen and tried to convince you how important this is and what an honor it would be to come here ... but ... something went wrong. Changes that normally take weeks took only hours with you. I expected to have more time to ease you into what was going to happen. Before I could explain everything you needed to know, you were shown the door, well before you were made ready. I knew, or at least thought I knew, what would happen to you the moment you went through without being mentally prepared, and I was terrified. I wasn't sure at first, but I soon realized that things were different with you. When I came through myself, you were in a heavy sleep, and again, your changes happened more rapidly than they should have. The changes that should have gradually occurred continued to happen rapidly while you slept these past few weeks."

"Weeks! Weeks!? I have been here for weeks!?" yelled Angela.

"Hold on. Don't get excited. Time runs differently here. You have been here for weeks, but you have only been gone from home for a very short time."

"What do you mean?" asked Angela, again regaining her composure. "How much time?"

"I will get to that. You need too much information for me to skip around. Here's what was supposed to happen. After I decided that you were capable of what was to come, and had prepared you to start your training, we would go through the door together. I was going to tell you about the plan the night we had dinner, but I had no idea how much you had changed and figured I could wait a bit longer. You are just too young, and I knew the process was going to be hard. I should have told you then, since I knew that you had the stone, and that the process must have begun. I was sure you would be looking for answers. I'm sorry that I stayed quiet, but I needed more information before I tried to explain."

Raven reached under her tunic and pulled out a similar stone and said, "That shock that surged through your body was a catalyst for the changes you experienced over the few days that followed. The final change is different for everyone, based on his or her own attributes, but there are similarities as well. I assume that your strength and endurance have increased, and that your senses have strengthened."

"Most of my senses," commented Angela. "My sense of smell is the only thing that has not seemed to change."

"Interesting," pondered Raven. "I guess that makes sense. Anyway, another factor that delayed my assistance was the interruption by our friend whom you saw in the woods."

"How do you know about that? Were you there?" questioned Angela.

"He was following you. He followed you to my house that night, which is why I wanted you to stay with me. I have been following you ever since that day, and when you went into the woods -- and we will be talking about why you would do something so stupid later -- I followed you in, and apparently so did he."

"Then did you see the fight? Did you see what was fighting him? Who was that!?" asked Angela.

Raven smiled, "I was the one you saw fighting him."

"What do you mean? The thing I saw fighting him was ..." Angela trailed off.

Raven took a step back, and before Angela's eyes, she changed into the creature that Angela had seen in the woods.

Raven's black sleek feathers grew from her skin and the angles of her face changed. Her hands grew into talons, and finally two large wings grew from her back. The clothes that she wore seemed to allow for the change easily.

"It was me," said Raven.

"How did you do that!? You can change back!?" exclaimed Angela.

Raven smiled. "As I was saying, we were interrupted, and I couldn't decide whether I should continue with my plan to make you ready for today, or if I should hold off. I needed to find out more about him, and I have. We will talk more about him another time."

Angela wanted to protest, but she was finding it hard to speak at that moment. If she hadn't known Ms. Cray so well, she would have been scared. Well, at least Angela thought she knew her. In addition, Angela felt that she was getting some of the answers she needed and didn't want to do anything to make that flow of information stop.

Raven continued, "Back to your new necklace. As I said before, this stone is your connection to this place, but it is also a connection to me since I have one as well. I'll show you what I mean. Take the stone and hold it tight in your hand. Now think of a color." Angela did as she was told. "Purple," said Raven.

"That's the color I was thinking about!" returned Angela.

"With more practice, we will be able to speak to each other through our minds as long as we both have our stones. I need you to make sure that you understand something important. You should never tell the things I've told you to anyone else unless absolutely necessary, and even then only after consulting with me. Your life may depend on keeping this all a secret."

"How come no matter what I did to lose the stone it always seemed to come back?" asked Angela.

"That is a good question, but I am not entirely sure how it works. We are able to move from here to home through a portal. I think this stone uses the same concept to move to wherever you are. Just remember to always keep it safe and secret. Once the stone started the changes to your body, you became connected to it. You can no easier lose your hand than that stone."

"So that door is a portal?" asked Angela.

"Yes," said Raven, "If you had been properly prepared by me, we would have gone through the portal together, but instead you were able to use the door on your own. You shouldn't have been able to even see the door, let alone go through it. I saw the picture of the door in the dark room and took it just to be safe. I didn't think you could see the door in the photo, but I didn't want to take any chances since I had yet to prepare you for it."

Angela thought for a moment and said, "I was wondering what happened to the photo. You know how sometimes you glance at something out of the corner of your eye, but when you look you don't see anything? It was kind of like that. Every time I passed by the common room, I would get a sense of something different, but when I looked around, there would be nothing different that I could see. Then I took that photo of a group of people in the common room during the yearbook meeting. I noticed something different about it, but couldn't pinpoint anything in particular. So I made a bigger photo from the negative. I didn't have room for it on my line so Emma put it with hers. It took me a long time to realize what I was seeing, but I finally saw the door in the photo.

After that, I felt this force drawing me through the door. When I went through, I heard you behind me."

"I didn't stop to think that there might have been a copy when I took the original. There are rules about the doorways, and it looks like someone, or something, was able to break one of those rules using your interest in photography. I will have to think about that. What we really need to figure out is who manipulated you into finding that door so soon, and why," said Raven.

"What about figuring out what has happened to me?" asked Angela as she held up her new talons. "What is going on with me?" asked Angela, as her eyes welled up with tears again.

"This place changes you, based on your personality and strengths, and it obviously had a pretty good idea about you before you came."

"What do you mean?" said Angela.

Raven answered, "This place takes certain traits in each of us and finds the best fit. For instance, you have a love for the dark and the night time. You have an excellent head on your shoulders. In fact, you look a bit like an owl now. As far as my situation, you have seen my gift for gab, and, though I hate to brag, I have a pretty high IQ. There are other things about me as well, that I'm not quite ready to share, but given all of those characteristics, I resemble a raven or a crow."

"So your name is Raven Cray, very close to Raven Crow. I take it that was not your given name."

"No. I have had many names; you tend to get creative over the years."

"You also seem to collect things like a magpie," remarked Angela.

"Yep, I probably have a little magpie in me as well. It's not always a perfect match," replied Raven.

Angela stopped listening for a minute and turned to the creek to look at her reflection again. "I *do* look like an owl, don't I?"

It was more of a statement than a question but Raven answered just the same, "Looks that way. That is why your sense of smell hasn't changed, since owls have a poor sense of smell."

They both sat for a moment staring at their reflections. Raven wanted to give Angela some time to absorb everything she had said.

A few minutes passed and Raven asked, "What are you feeling right now, Angela?"

"I'm not sure what to think. I liked my life the way it was, now that I have finally accepted the loss of my dad. I think back over this last week and I still have so many questions, but I guess it all comes down to this one: why is this all happening?"

"You're right. That is the big question. That is the one question I was hoping to avoid today because it is the question that scares me the most. The truth of the matter is, I'm not really sure. For as long as I can remember there has only been one other like us, and he was the one who trained me. Although I didn't know it at the time, he was training me to be his replacement; he was very old when I was chosen. There is still a great deal that I do not know, but I do know that there is and should always be at least one of us. The fact that you are with me now is scarier than what I fought in the woods."

"I don't understand. Why?" asked Angela.

Raven answered, "Because I am not here to train you to be my replacement. Whatever I, and those who had come before me, have been awaiting all these years may be coming now. I am hoping that we will be able to find out the answer to that question before that 'reason why' is upon us."

"Well, at least I'm glad you are not training me to be your replacement." Angela paused and then asked, "What did you do with your training?"

"That too is a good question. At first I trained very hard and asked the same 'why' questions that you asked. My predecessor could not answer my questions either. He just told me that we needed to be ready for whatever came."

"And did anything ever come?" asked Angela.

"It did the other night in the woods," answered Raven.

"And you are sure I am not supposed to replace you?" asked Angela.

"Don't worry. The one who trained me was very old. He knew that his time would be coming to an end one day soon. No, you are stuck with me for a long time. At least, I hope so." Raven grinned again. With the blink of an eye she turned back into the Ms. Cray that Angela had always known.

"That was amazing!" exclaimed Angela. "Will I be able to change back and forth like that!?"

"I hope so; if you can't you are going to look funny at the grocery store!" laughed Raven. "You see, you are Angela and now you are also ... we are going to have to come up with a new name for you. For now we will stick with Angela. Anyway, you are both Angela and this owl. You can be either, or even both. You just need to focus."

Angela tried. She focused on what she normally looked like as hard as she could, but nothing happened.

"Don't worry, you'll get it. For now, let's focus on where we are."

"That's my next question. Where are we? Are we close to Gap? How do we get back?"

"As I said earlier, we are both far away and also close to Gap. That question is a lesson all in itself. For now, I will just say that the doorway to get back to Gap is in that cave over there. As far as where we are, it will be easier to show you later tonight."

"Later tonight? How long are we staying? I need to get back and talk to my mom. I don't want to even think about what she is going through right now. With all those kids disappearing ... Emma! We need to go find Emma!" Angela turned to look at the cave and was ready to sprint over there when Raven touched her arm.

"Hold on. First things first. I know what Jane told you. Before you went through the doorway, I tracked down Jane and persuaded her to tell me everything she told you. We can't just go off looking for Emma without first giving you proper training. You need to understand fully what has happened to you. Just remember, you can't even change back to your human form yet; are you just going to run through the school covered in feathers? Second, your mom has not come back from her trip yet. I said before that time is different here, and in the weeks that you have been here, only a few minutes have passed at home. I don't think Emma has been hurt just yet. Judging from what I have seen, I think that creature was looking for you and found Emma instead. I think he may be the reason kids have been disappearing; I think he is collecting them. I just don't know why." Angela began to protest but Raven stopped her. "Trust me, I know a collection when I see one."

Remembering back to Ms. Cray's house, Angela was forced to agree.

"We have time to think this through and at least start your training before we have to rush off and get into trouble."

Angela started to speak again, but Raven cut her off. "Enough questions for now. Let everything sink in while we begin our training."

"Wait. I just have one more thing to ask," said Angela. "What if this is too much for me and I don't want to do it?"

Raven stared at her for a moment and spoke with great kindness, "You will always have a choice. Your will is your own; but before you choose to walk away, spend some time with me and I will show you what it is you are being asked to do. Get all the information first, let me train you, and then we will find Emma. When we've finished those things, you can decide what you would like to do and I will respect your decision. Fair enough?"

Angela stared into Raven's eyes and saw nothing but compassion. "Fair enough," answered Angela. "Show me what I need to know."

7

HOME AWAY FROM HOME

Angela looked around the clearing. Now that she had decided to stay, she wanted to see where she was going to be spending her time. The grotto was very large; it seemed to be almost the size of a football field. Very tall trees surrounded the grotto on all sides and on the left side, the creek wound in and out of the woods. At the end of the grotto, the creek seemed to make a right turn around a bend of trees. The trees were too thick along that side to see through, so she couldn't tell what was around the bend; and the clouds were so low that the tops of the taller trees were hidden. Behind her lay the cave where she had been told she had come into this grotto. It was too dark to see what was inside that cave.

"So tell me about this place. How long are we going to stay here?" asked Angela.

"Well," answered Raven, "we will be here until you have learned what you need to know. As for this place, it has always been called the grove. This is where we will live and train as long as we are here. There are different areas in the grove that lend themselves to different training. We will have plenty of fruit and vegetables to eat, and if you choose, we can even hunt," said Raven.

"Hunt? Like deer?" returned Angela.

"Something like that. For now, I will show you where to find the easy food. I am sure you are hungry."

Before Angela had a chance to respond, her stomach growled. Until Raven said something, she hadn't even noticed how hungry she was.

"The water here tastes very sweet. Try it." Angela did and smiled.

"Come over here."

Raven led Angela along the bank of the creek to the edge of the woods. As they stepped into the wooded area, Angela found herself surrounded by trees. They were not as thick here as in the rest of the jungle, and there were strange bushes scattered throughout. In one of the trees she saw another strange-looking squirrel.

"What is that?" asked Angela as she followed it.

"That? It's a squirrel," answered Raven.

"That isn't like any squirrel I have ever seen!" observed Angela as she followed it around the tree.

"No, the squirrels around here are a little different," said Raven, as she started picking some fruit.

"A little different! It has two tails!" exclaimed Angela.

"Yep, it's yellow, too," smiled Raven.

"That's all I get? 'It's yellow!?' Where *are* we?" asked Angela.

"We will get to that later. Help me pick some of this fruit," said Raven as she turned to another tree.

Angela realized that she was not going to get any more answers just now, so she took another look around. She found that she was surrounded by what looked like apple trees, but the fruit did not look like apples; it looked more like large kiwi. The skin looked tougher and had a light green color. Raven grabbed one of the fruits and tossed it to Angela, who took a big bite. The fruit tasted like a cross between a pear and a kiwi. A huge smile stretched across Angela's face as the juice dripped down her chin. Angela proceeded to eat two more.

"Not too many on your first day! Come with me," laughed Raven.

They moved off together to the side of the fruit glen, and Raven led Angela to the large bushes among the trees. The bushes had what looked like potatoes hanging from them.

"I thought that potatoes grew in the ground," puzzled Angela.

"These are not ordinary potatoes. Help me gather some up. These are better when they are cooked; we can have them later for dinner." Raven also picked some leaves from various plants that she pointed out to Angela.

"These will add some nice flavor to the stew."

Raven pulled what looked like wild onions from the ground, as well as some strange-looking green carrots.

Raven led Angela to another type of tree that had branches which were covered with a very odd-shaped nut.

"Try one of these. They are very filling," said Raven.

Angela caught a nut as Raven tossed it into the air, and popped it into her mouth.

"It tastes like steak!" raved Angela. "What is this nut called?"

"Actually, I have no idea what any of these things are called. They just started growing here within the last few years. I call these steak nuts, for obvious reasons."

"All these plants just started growing?" asked Angela.

"Well, over the last twenty years or so," answered Raven.

"Wait. Over the last twenty years? I'm sorry, I know it is not polite to ask, but I need to know now. How old are you?"

"Ah ... well, a lady never reveals ..." Raven laughed. "I'm just kidding. I am seventy-three years old."

"What!? You can't be serious!" exclaimed Angela.

"Aging well is one of the best and worst perks of our upgrades."

"What do you mean?" asked Angela.

"We need to always be at the peak of our physical condition, so we age much slower than everyone else. The problem is that you tend to outlive all your friends and family."

Angela thought about that idea for a moment. She could see the advantages and disadvantages to living so long. She decided not to dwell on the idea just yet. There was too much to process to focus on one thing for too long.

Angela ate a few more steak nuts and followed Raven back to the grove.

"Now that you have eaten, let me give you a little tour," said Raven.

Across from the fruit and nut trees was another group of trees that were oddly shaped. If Angela didn't know better, she would say that the trees were a jungle gym that had been made to look like trees. As the two of them got closer, she could see that this group of trees was much bigger then she had first thought. Not only did this group have branches at different levels, there seemed to be a complete obstacle course, all made from growing trees. There were balance beams, uneven bars and even thick areas to climb. The obstacle course seemed to go far along the side of the grove, almost all the way to the bend that blocked Angela's view.

"You are going to spend a lot of time here," smiled Raven. "This area is where we are going to start your training. First we will see how fast you are, and how good your endurance is. Then we will see how much better you can become."

Angela groaned, "Looks a lot like gym to me!"

"When I am done with you, you're going to miss gym!" returned Raven.

They continued to walk down the grove towards the bend. A short distance from the end of the endurance track, as Angela had observed earlier, the creek had come back out of the woods and turned back in again. Here the creek bed had widened a great deal, taking on the appearance of a large pond. Sticking out of the surface of the creek were many logs, pointing straight up. They were all of different diameters and were relatively close together, reaching different heights.

"What is that?" Angela said as she pointed to the water.

"That's another training ground. That one focuses on balance and agility."

Angela's stomach turned as she said, "Balance has never been my friend. I have a feeling I am going to be getting wet."

"Me, too," smiled Raven.

Angela looked back toward the cave. She stared at the mountain, again realizing how high it rose. Then something dawned on her.

"Can I ask you a question?" asked Angela.

"Sure," returned Raven.

"Not that I am looking for more complications in my life, but I noticed there is a big difference between you and me," observed Angela.

"Let me guess: wings?" asked Raven.

"Yep, wings," replied Angela.

"Don't worry," replied Raven. "You are still going through changes. Your body needs to adjust slowly. Give it some time and I am sure they will come. Mine did not appear right away, either. In the meantime, I need to show you where we are going to sleep."

Raven led Angela back down the grove and around the bend. On either side of the wide lane were thick bushes with large red flowers. The clouds had finally burned off with the morning sun and at the end of the field was something Angela couldn't believe: the largest and strangest tree that she had ever seen. Shaped unlike any tree she had ever seen before, it was as tall as a skyscraper. It formed a column of giant deep green leaves, some almost ten feet across. The branches wove and bent to take on the shape of a huge column that went as high as Angela could see. As she walked closer, the fragrance assaulted her and she swooned as the incredible smell coming from the tree entranced her. The scent reminded her of flowers and spring. As the two got closer, it became apparent that she was seeing something that in all actuality should not exist, but her senses were telling her otherwise. Angela reached out her hand toward a giant leaf and it moved slightly to accept her touch. That alone took her by surprise. When she felt the leaf she saw that it had the same texture as any other leaf she had felt but was easily six inches thick (or wide?). She also noticed tiny filaments that gently wrapped around her fingers like a friendly embrace as she moved them across the leaf's surface. A feeling of great calm took over her while she touched the tree, as if the grace and serenity of the tree had passed into her.

"Raven, this is absolutely the most incredible thing I have ever seen!" As the words came from her mouth, the feeling coming from the tree turned to a sense of smugness, and happiness.

"Stop," said Raven, "You are going to give her a big head."

"Her?" said Angela. "How do you know?"

"After a while you just sense it. Can you sense her now?"

"I think so. I feel happiness coming from her. Just before that, I felt a calm sensation."

"That would be the tree," said Raven, smiling. "I'm glad you like her. This is where we will live while we are here, but there is a catch."

"What's that?"

Raven smiled and took two giant steps forward and spread her huge black wings. With one flap she rose into the sky. About fifteen feet up, she hovered in mid-air, turned, and said, "You need to get to the top. See you there!"

And with that she flew straight up to towards the top of the tree. Angela stood there, dumbfounded. Finally, she sighed and walked to the base of the tree. With a promise to herself not to look down, she began to climb.

About three hundred feet into her climb, Angela broke her promise. Surprisingly, the view did not bother her as she had expected it would. In fact, the higher she got, the more comfortable she became. She assumed that the tree was helping with that sensation. At first, every handhold needed to be secure before she moved an inch, but as she got comfortable she found that jumping from branch to branch was as natural to her as walking. Her advanced senses started to kick in again and she found that each of those senses made her even more adept at climbing. She could feel the strength of the branches, and the filaments of the leaves grabbing hold and releasing at the exact perfect moments. She could see what branch could hold her by instantly examining the cracks in the old wood. In the beginning of her climb it wasn't really necessary, since the lower branches were as thick as huge trees themselves, but as she got closer to the top she would work her way to the edge of the branches to get a look at the land around her. Raven was being very elusive as to where they were, so Angela had hoped to get an idea by looking at the land around her. She worked her way to the end of one of the branches so she could see beyond the thick cover of leaves. Finally, at the edge, she could see. In the distance was the mountain that she had seen before. The size of that mountain was astonishing even in comparison to the tree. In every other direction there was only a vast forest. The creek she had drunk from could be seen leading to a river that was so wide it could be mistaken for a lake. 'Is everything around here super-sized?' thought Angela.

When Angela was done admiring the view, she turned to press on. Her new talons, and the strength she was able to put behind them, made them the ultimate in climbing tools. Her hands and feet rarely slipped and if so, they regained their grip quickly and easily, especially since branches would sometimes move to make her climb a bit easier.

After what seemed like three hours of climbing, Angela could see a large platform ahead. Carefully, Angela climbed alongside the platform and jumped down to land gracefully in the center. The wood platform seemed to grow out from the tree. She could see that it was placed in a way so it would be easy to leave the platform and glide directly into the sky, if you could fly. The wide platform led into a wall of leaves towards the center of the tree. Looking up, Angela could tell that there was still quite some distance to the top of the tree. Angela walked down the platform and parted the wall of leaves to peer through. Even after all she had seen and all that she had experienced, nothing prepared her for what lay before her.

There were no leaves in the center of the tree for as far up as she could see, and instead of having random branches, the tree had grown levels of rooms and stairways. The stairs curved and twisted all around the tremendous trunk of the tree, leading in all different directions, to many different platforms. Each platform led to a level of paths that led to more rooms that also grew from the tree. At first it all looked very random and confused but as Angela studied what she saw, she realized that each area was perfectly organized in what would be best described as floors, all circling the trunk. This tree could easily house thousands of people, but that was what was missing. There were no people. It seemed as if this city in the tree was missing all its inhabitants, save for one. Standing on one of the platforms two levels up was Raven, in all her feathers and glory.

As she walked up the stairs to meet Raven, Angela looked into the rooms that she passed. Many of the rooms held furniture, most of which seemed to grow from the walls and floors of the rooms. It was as if the tree knew the needs of those that it housed and grew to accommodate everything that they required.

"What do you think?" asked Raven.

Angela turned with a start. "It is incredible! I was amazed by the grove, and how beautiful that was, but I could never imagine a place like this in my wildest dreams. It is just so incredible!"

"I have explored so many rooms here, but I don't think that even I have seen them all, even after all these years."

"Who lives here?" asked Angela.

"Right now, just us," answered Raven.

"But there are so many rooms. Where are all the people?"

"As long as I have been here there were only ever two of us, and then just me. Considering that this platform is the lowest point of all the rooms, the people that lived here must have been like us, and able to fly up here," said Raven.

"I know birds at home build their nests up high for protection. Since this tree is really as high as it gets, what did they need protection from? And was it enough, considering that they are no longer here?" considered Angela.

"If they were chased off, you would think there would have been things left behind. But each room looks as if no one ever lived here. There are no personal items, no artwork, no writings, not anything to indicate that someone ever lived here. Even if it was years ago, there would be something. Even archaeologists found tools and pottery of ancient humans. Here is a complete city in the sky and there is nothing but what grew from the tree. There are rooms that definitely serve certain purposes -- kitchens, bathrooms, even libraries-- but they are all completely empty," said Raven.

"It seems like every question that I get answered leads to three more questions that are even more baffling," mumbled Angela.

"Fortunately, there is enough to learn to keep you busy for now. I'll show you where I am staying and the rooms I picked out for you. You will be close to me, but not so close that you won't get a little privacy. I also brought some things from home to make you more comfortable," said Raven as she led Angela up a set of stairs.

After a few minutes of climbing, they reached a set of rooms. Angela was pleased to find several items from her room back home, especially a few of her cameras.

"Hey, this is the one I had when I went through the door!" exclaimed Angela.

"I thought you would be happy to see that camera. I am going to let you look around and get settled. Once you're ready, come find me and we can get some dinner. We can start training in the morning."

With that comment, Raven spread her wings and glided across to another platform. From there, she followed a set of stairs that led around the trunk. Angela made note of where she had gone, and turned to look at her room.

Like all the other rooms in the area, Angela's room was mostly open, having walls on only three sides and only leaves for a ceiling. The room was not really big; it was only about fifteen feet across and eight feet deep. In the room were a table and two chairs that seemed to grow out of the floor. There were shelves built into the walls that held some of the things from her room back home. Along the back wall there was a doorway that Angela hadn't seen when she first walked in. This doorway lead to a second room that was more private. It was the same size across as the first room, but four feet deeper. This room contained a bed and another table and chairs, and, just like the furniture in the other room, everything was growing from the tree. On the shelves in this room were only a few items of clothing, and only some were from home. Mostly, these shelves held clothes similar to the clothes that Raven wore. At that moment, Angela realized that not only did she not have any clothes on, she no longer had any of her feathers! She had turned back into her old self. She hadn't realized when it happened, so she was not quite sure how she had done it. After the mega climb she realized that she was pretty gross. She could really use a bathroom. Just then she saw a curtain in the corner of her room that sectioned off part of the room. Pushing the curtain aside, she saw what she was looking for: a bathroom! The fixtures were a little strange, but the room had what she needed. The toilet was much longer than she was used to; she figured the longer size was to accommodate her wings. In the corner of the room, a large wooden basin on the floor looked like an oversized sink. Above the sink were several small holes in the ceiling and a large knot on the back wall. Without thinking, she reached for the knot and when she touched it, water started to fall from the ceiling into the basin. What a cool thing! Taking advantage of the water, she stepped into the basin and noticed a small shelf that held a bottle of shampoo and soap in brands she recognized from Raven's house. Twenty minutes later, Angela felt like herself again.

Angela dressed in her favorite sweats and T-shirt from home, grabbed her camera, and took some shots to show Emma. She knew that she would not be allowed to show anyone else these pictures. Her stomach dropped when she thought about Emma, who was her only motivation right now. Since it was starting to get dark, Angela wanted to set out to find Raven and see what they could have to eat. Angela's eyes were just as good in the dark as they were in the light, so she didn't worry about setting out at night, but she wasn't sure exactly where Raven had gone. She went up the stairs that Raven had ascended, and didn't have far to go. As she got to the top of the stairs, Angela could see the light from a set of rooms up ahead. Raven had several candles spread throughout her space, and Angela noticed that Raven's rooms had the same layout as her own. The only difference was all the little collectables and figurines that were spread out on every shelf. Angela giggled. Raven was more like a crow than she probably realized, with all the shiny things spread all over.

"I see you are back to the old you and you found the shower!" exclaimed Raven.

"I am and I did, although I have no idea how I did it," answered Angela.

"What were you doing when you changed?" asked Raven.

"I was thinking about my old life as I was looking at the stuff you brought for me and then ... no feathers," answered Angela.

"That may be the trigger to change back to your human form, but can you feather out again?" asked Raven.

Angela thought for a minute but couldn't figure out how to regain her feathers. "I'm not sure. What should I focus on to change back?"

"That, my dear, you are going to need to figure out for yourself. It's not that I don't want to tell you, but what makes me go bird is not what will make you change. It will come to you soon enough. For now, let's get something to eat."

Raven took Angela back down the stairs and over to another room. This room was central to the other rooms in the area and was very open. The circular structure was more like an area than an enclosed room. It reminded Angela of a large round mushroom with several openings to enter. Between each doorway the walls had shelves full of different pots and pans. The brand names on the pots led Angela to believe that Raven had brought them from home. There were also many sinks that were similar in design to the shower in Angela's room. In the center of the room was a large fire. The smoke drifted up and out of a large hole in the ceiling, and was trapped there by a long hollow branch like a chimney. Over the fire hung a large pot that was full of stew.

Angela was starving and didn't waste much time before diving into a huge bowl of stew.

"Your appetite's still on overdrive, huh? It will slow back down soon enough. In the meantime, enjoy the fact that you can eat anything you want without gaining a pound," said Raven with a smile.

"If my appetite doesn't slow down soon, I'm going to eat my mom out of house and home," replied Angela as she sat back from finishing her third helping.

"Don't worry; it will. I want to show you something after you're done washing the dishes," said Raven as she got up to leave. "I'll meet you outside."

Angela found that the sinks did work just like her shower. It was amazing how the water seemed to come out of the wood. When Angela was done with the dishes, she met Raven outside.

"Follow me. I want to answer one of your questions now," said Raven.

"What question is that?" asked Angela

"The one about where we are," answered Raven. "Follow me."

Raven led them to another stairway that cut through to a walkway. This was wider than most of the other walkways and led straight through the tree. It took quite some time to walk through the tree, but eventually they came out on the other side of the tree to another large platform.

"There are several of these wider walkways. Each of them leads straight through the tree," said Raven.

"What did you bring me here to see?" asked Angela.

Raven didn't say anything; she only pointed into the sky. After orienting herself to where Raven was pointing, Angela could see it: a blue sphere. By the shape of the continents, Angela realized she was a lot farther from home than she had thought.

"Is that what I think it is?" asked Angela.

"Yep, home sweet home. That's the Earth. You and I are on another planet," answered Raven.

"I don't understand. What planet could we possibly be on that is so close to ours? I know I slept through a lot of school, but I think I would remember if there was a planet that we could live on this close by," said Angela.

"That's the thing. 'They' have not found this planet yet. From what I have been told, it has always been here, but in a slightly different time. It's called Avaria," said Raven.

"Avaria? And what do you mean, 'a different time?'" asked Angela.

"Well, that is the best way to explain it, even if it is not entirely accurate. It seems that this planet is out of phase with our planet. It is here, but something is shielding it from Earth's view, and I think that whatever is doing the shielding is messing with time and space. I don't completely understand how or why, but I know that I can spend months on this planet and when I return, only a few hours have passed back on Earth."

"So we can see Earth because only this planet is shielded?" asked Angela.

"That is my guess. The only way to see this planet is to travel through one of the doorways. Not only do we cover a great distance when we go through a door, but I think we also change the timeframe in which we exist."

"So, basically, this planet is out of phase with the rest of the galaxy?" asked Angela.

"That is the best way to look at it. You are handling this pretty well,' said Raven.

"After waking up and finding your body covered with feathers, everything else seems pretty mild."

Raven laughed. "You have had more than enough for one day. Get to bed and we will start your training in the morning."

Raven and Angela worked their way back to their rooms. Angela was still awe struck with everything she saw. Strange animals were jumping through the trees, and she still couldn't get over the size of the tree they were walking through. So many things were going around in Angela's head that it was hard to sleep. Much of this was very confusing and she had a hard time grasping it all. Finally, exhaustion got the best of her and she fell asleep.

8

TRAINING DAY

The sun broke through the windows in Angela's room
early the next morning. The room's rounded windows, located
on three of the walls, looked like port holes; they did not have
glass, nor were there any coverings or curtains to block the
sun. The sun coming into the room worked better than both
of Angela's alarm clocks back home. She pulled herself out of
bed, thankful for the mattress and bedding that Raven must
have brought for her. The hard wood frame would not have
made for a pleasant night's sleep on its own. Angela got up
and stretched. She could feel the previous day's climb in her
arms and legs as she walked over to the table and sat down.
On the table was a picture of her and her mom in a small
frame, which Raven must have brought over as well. It was a
picture that Angela had had for a long time but rarely looked
at. As she looked at the photo now, she wondered what her
mom was doing and what she would say if she knew what was

happening to her daughter. Angela began to miss her mother very much.

Angela got up from the table, and went to wash her face, brush her teeth, and put on the clothes that Raven had brought for her. It took her a minute to figure out how to put the tunic on, but it did wrap around her in a way that seemed conducive to having wings. After several tugs and adjustments she was satisfied that she had it on correctly. If she did figure out how to change back into her feather form, she could tell this tunic would be comfortable and easy to move around in. Angela then walked into the front room of her little cottage and looked outside. The temperature was very comfortable -- she guessed it was about 75 degrees --and there was a slight breeze. It felt like a warm spring day. As always, Angela had awoken very hungry. Listening to the rumbling in her stomach, she grabbed one of her digital cameras and went to the kitchen, where she had had dinner the previous night. In the kitchen, she found a tray full of fruit and a note. 'When you're done eating, meet me by the cave. Raven.' Angela picked up one piece of fruit after another and before long the tray was empty. She then began her long climb down to the glade, stopping every so often to take a picture or two.

Without her talons and increased strength, the climb was much more difficult, and she had to be more careful than before. She also noticed that she was getting tired more quickly than she did on the way up. Looked like Angela 3.0 was an even better upgrade, if only she could figure out how to turn it on! As she carefully worked her way down, she kept an eye out for Raven. Finally, after a few hours, she reached the ground, exhausted. She walked across the grotto and saw Raven by the obstacle course she had seen yesterday.

"It took you long enough! You look tired, too!" exclaimed Raven as she handed Angela a canteen of water.

"I was a lot faster yesterday. I need to be able to change," answered Angela before taking a long pull on the water.

"I agree, but in the meantime you need to train this body as well. You need to train both forms because you will not always have the luxury of changing. You don't ever want to be defenseless," said Raven.

"I can't help but notice the sense of urgency in your voice. The way you talk it sounds as though we are going to be attacked at any moment," noticed Angela.

"From this point on, you must assume that you are always under some type of threat. That way, you cannot be taken by surprise. The training you are about to receive is very serious and will now be your first priority to learn. Let's begin now."

Raven led Angela to the beginning of the strange tree obstacle course.

"As you can see, this is an obstacle course. It's pretty straightforward; you start on this end and you race to that end," said Raven, gesturing to the end of the course.

"You're a wealth of instruction," laughed Angela.

"I'm pretty sure you will figure it out as you go," smiled Raven. "At first, just work your way through; we will start timing you later."

Angela looked at the course, which didn't look that difficult to her. The branches were laid out in a way that would require her to jump, crawl, climb and sprint. There were even some sections that seemed to require balance and agility. Before she changed, she would have had a difficult time, but now, even though the course was pretty long -- Angela guessed about fifty yards -- it seemed pretty straightforward.

"Any time now," said Raven.

"Got it," and with that, Angela bolted. She loved her new speed and wanted to impress Raven. She jumped over the first set of branches, which required her to jump about four feet into the air. She was impressed with how easily she soared over them. The next group of branches forced her to go low, but instead of dropping to her belly, she jumped into a dive and rolled under the branches. At this point, Angela was getting a little full of herself. The following set of branches was another jump. Again, Angela positioned herself for the easy jump, but this time something was off. What should have been a very direct jump, not half as high as the last, landed Angela on her face. Thanks to her increased reflexes, her pride was hurt more than anything else. Surprisingly, Raven was right there and helped Angela to her feet.

"That was really impressive, up until the face plant," jeered Raven.

"I'm not sure what happened. I was sure I was high enough to make that jump," said Angela.

"Okay, let's try it again," said Raven.

Angela sighed and brushed herself off while she set off for the beginning of the course. This time she was going to be more careful. Angela set off again at a sprint, but not as quickly as the last run. Again she moved through the course with great dexterity. As she approached the jump she had missed the last time, she was careful to make sure she would clear the branches. This time everything went as planned. The next jump she approached was almost the same height. As she launched herself again, she looked forward to see what was next and her foot caught the top of the branch, again causing her to go down hard. Angela looked up and used Raven's hand to pull herself up again.

"I don't understand. I was careful to clear that jump," said Angela, clearly frustrated.

"You need to open all your senses, Angela. You are assuming too much. Do it again, but this time pay more attention to your surroundings. Keep in mind that you are now an extraordinary person. You will need something a bit out of the ordinary to train on. Go back to the beginning."

"I *was* paying attention," grumbled Angela under her breath. She brushed off the dirt again and started back toward the beginning of the course. This time, she took the course a little slower and watched everything she could. Again the first two obstacles were easy and as she approached the third she readied herself for the jump. She watched all around her and what she saw surprised her almost as much as the previous fall. As she left the ground, the trees that made up the wall moved, raising the wall she was trying to clear so that it became six inches higher. She had never seen a tree move before, and the shock of it almost threw her off yet again, but paying more attention to her surroundings meant that she was ready. Instead of jumping to clear the obstacle, she jumped to land on top. Her angle allowed her to grab the top of the wall and pivot over using the momentum of the rising wall to push her over the top. With a feeling of triumph in her heart, she readied herself to jump down from the wall and continue to the next obstacle. Before she could pounce, a branch came from nowhere and knocked her back off the obstacle, down to the ground, flat on her back. Angela yelled in frustration and Raven once again helped her to her feet.

"Got a better idea what you're up against now?" asked Raven.

"Yeah, a bunch of crazy trees that cheat! You could have let me know ahead of time," answered Angela.

"And miss out on a chance to teach you a great lesson? Not to mention the ten point landings! This course is meant to show you that not everything is as it seems. In every situation you find yourself, you must always keep your eyes open and expect the unexpected. Again," said Raven, pointing to the beginning.

So Angela once again started the obstacle course. This time she was better prepared and made a great deal of progress before she was knocked to the ground. She had made it very far this time and was confident that on her next attempt she would be successful. When she had gone back to the beginning of the course, she exploded into a fast sprint, hoping to finally make it through, when she saw that all the branches had moved. The course was completely different than it had been the time before!

"This is impossible!" yelled Angela as she lay on her back on the ground, this time refusing to get up, even with Raven's help. "How are you supposed to finish this course when it keeps changing?!"

Raven smiled, but not in a jeering way; she showed understanding and sympathy.

"You have been at it for hours. Let's get some lunch."

At that point, Angela realized how hungry she was and followed Raven to the area of trees that produced all the fruits and vegetables. Every bite seemed to fill Angela's aching muscles with energy and healing.

"Are you ready for another go?" asked Raven.

"I guess," replied Angela.

So the afternoon followed, with much of the same activity as had filled the morning. Angela was pleased with her progress, even though she never completed the course. Raven finally pulled up a dirty, sweaty, determined Angela and dusted off her clothes.

"You have had enough for one day. You can start again in the morning," said Raven. "What!? Stop now!? I almost made it!" protested Angela.

"It will be dark soon and you have a long climb ahead of you. It is going to take you longer unless you figure out how to feather out on the way up." With that statement, Raven jumped straight up, opened her wings, and took to the air. The beautiful black wings seemed to fold out of nowhere. Angela watched Raven fly out of sight, around the bend towards the tree. She looked down at herself, hoping to see feathers, and was disappointed again.

'Well,' thought Angela, 'I guess it could be worse.' Not exactly sure how, she started for the tree.

Hours later, Angela dragged herself up onto the platform and lay flat on her back. Every part of her body hurt more than it had ever hurt in her life. Even with the stronger physique she now possessed, she was ready to pass out right there on the hard, cold wood. She dragged herself up, though, and made her way to her room to crash into her shower. She scrubbed off what seemed like two inches of grime and sweat and put on her comfy sweats and a T shirt. Not sure what to do with her dirty clothes, she brought them outside and put them in an empty room next to hers. They smelled too nasty to keep them near her bed. She then lay down on her bed, intending to rest for only a moment, and drifted instantly to sleep. An hour later she was nudged back awake.

"Ten more minutes, Mom, please," groaned Angela.

"Dinner's ready," returned Raven. "I let you sleep for a little while, but you need to eat."

Angela and her stomach agreed. She tried to get up and found out her legs wouldn't work, and her arms were under full protest as well. "I don't think I can move," frowned Angela.

"I had a feeling you would say that. Your muscles have all tightened up. Here, take this cream and rub it into your sore muscles. It will do wonders," said Raven.

Angela took the cream and did as she was instructed. The relief was immediate. Angela was still sore, but everything worked as it was supposed to.

"This stuff is amazing. What is it?"

"Ah ... it's probably best that you don't ask. There is something here that ... um ... excretes it. I will show you later. In the meantime, let's get something to eat."

The two walked over to the kitchen area. On the far side, Angela could see Raven's clothes hanging on a vine being used as a clothesline. Angela figured that Raven had washed them in her bathroom and hung them there to dry. Angela planned to do the same before bed. Dinner was some form of grilled meat. Angela was not sure what kind of meat it was, but she loved it. Though it had the consistency of chicken, it was a bit sweeter. She had three helpings and then leaned back in her chair.

"I wish I could cook half as well as you do," sighed Angela.

"Don't worry; you're going to learn. You will need to take a turn here and there. For now, though, concentrate on your training. The cooking lessons will come later. And as for your training, it's time to get back to it."

"What? Now? I understand that we don't have a lot of time but I don't think that even my new body can take any more today," objected Angela.

"Don't worry. This training is for your mind, and we're going to complete it sitting down," comforted Raven. "Follow me."

Raven, in her Ms. Cray form, led Angela to one of the platforms that over looked the vast forests of the area. The two of them sat down, and Angela enjoyed a moment of listening to the bright and varied sounds of the creatures in and around the tree.

"This time, there will be no surprises about what you are going to do; it's time to work on honing your senses. I know that your sight has increased; you should be able to see great distances very clearly. Tonight I want you to focus on your hearing. I need you to sit here and listen to everything: listen to the bugs, the animals, the wind, the trees; everything."

Angela focused on all the sounds around her as she closed her eyes and opened her ears. She could feel her enhanced senses kicking in and the sounds of the area attacked her.

Raven must have seen the stress in her face since she whispered, "Easy ... let it all in, and don't try to focus on any one thing. Just absorb the sounds; your mind will sort them out."

Angela did as she was told and allowed the sounds to wash over her. Just like that day in school when she had been sitting in her homeroom, she was beginning to become overwhelmed. She was about to focus on turning off the chaos in her mind when she heard Raven's voice assuring her that she was going to be fine. Something in her brain then seemed to click, and the sounds began to sort themselves out. It felt as though she was in a crowded room and each person was coming in turn to talk to her. Though the sounds were still all there, it was easy to focus on each one individually. As she concentrated, she could more easily distinguish one sound from another and bring out each sound in her mind. She found that she could listen to one sound and filter all the other sounds out; but not completely. The sounds were still there, but they were no longer a distraction. It was like looking at a large painting while focusing on a small piece of it. The rest of the painting does not distract the viewer, but adds to the entire picture. Angela could hear a small animal moving through the leaves, then switch to the swoosh of wings as a bird flew far above. She could hear the leaves rustle around her, then the bright chirping of a bug. Angela spent more time moving from sound to sound and then finally opened her eyes again. This time, her hearing did not dull, but became part of her. She could feel the sensitivity change but not go away. She was afraid to speak when she realized that she was alone. Raven had left and she didn't even know it. 'Great sense of hearing,' she thought with a scoff. She made her way back to their living quarters, and found Raven in her room reading a book.

"There you are," said Raven with a smile. "I was about to come get you so you could get some sleep."

"I was surprised that you were gone. I thought you would have waited with me," said Angela.

"I sat with you for the first hour, but after that I decided to get some things done. That was two hours ago," answered Raven.

"You mean I was sitting there for three hours?! I didn't think I was there for more than ten minutes," exclaimed Angela.

"You certainly were, and I expect you to do that every night. You will find that your increased hearing will be more of an advantage than your better sight," instructed Raven.

"I am nervous that every minute I spend here, Emma is put in more danger," sighed Angela.

"I know you are concerned, but trust me, you will not be able to help her until you learn how to use the new gifts you have been given," answered Raven.

"New gifts ... or a curse?" asked Angela.

"I guess that is all in your perception, but let's not get so deep tonight. You need to sleep," said Raven, with a look of concern. With that, Angela bid Raven goodnight and went up to her room. Sleep came as soon as her head hit her pillow.

9

THE MIND'S PICTURE

Angela awoke the next morning with intense pain in all her muscles. Looking at the table in her room, she saw the cream that she had used the night before. She was thankful that Raven had brought her some more, but wished it were closer. She tried to get up from her bed but her legs gave out and she fell hard to the floor. 'At least I fell towards the cream,' she thought and proceeded to crawl to the table. After finishing with the cream and giving it some time to sink in, she was able to at least get up and splash some water on her face.

Just as it had the day before, the table held a plate of fruit and a note instructing her to meet Raven by the obstacle course. Angela moaned and took her time with her breakfast. Two and a half hours of a long climb brought her to the ground. She so wished that she had her wings, or even just a feather to give her some hope. She tried everything she could think of on the way down to make her 'feather out,' as Raven called it, but not one tiny feather could be found. 'How am I going to help Emma if I can't control myself?' thought Angela in disgust.

Raven stood by the obstacle course again. Angela knew what she had to do and didn't waste any time with small talk. She set herself at the entrance to the course and broke into a sprint. With her enhanced hearing now more under control, she was able to make out the sounds of the movement within the trees. Unlike the day before, she could now hear the trees move as she approached. There were many times when she was still caught off guard, but not as many as the day before. Finally, just before lunch, Angela actually completed the course. She couldn't believe it, and was completely elated with her success. Raven came ever and congratulated her. "Not bad for a newbie. It feels good, doesn't it?"

"It sure does! I didn't think I would ever finish!" answered Angela.

"Well," said Raven, "don't get too used to it. We will be coming right back here for timed runs. Finishing the course is a great first step, but now we are going to work on getting your time down."

Angela was too excited with her triumph to be upset at the prospect of many more runs. Happily, she followed Raven to a blanket on the ground that held some fruits and vegetables from the surrounding area. There were also some foods she recognized from home. It had been a few weeks since she had had watermelon, so she especially enjoyed eating it now.

After lunch, Raven made good on her promise of more obstacle runs. Angela's increased sense of hearing was a huge asset and she attributed her successful completion of four more runs to that alone. She didn't count the thirteen runs that failed. No sense in dwelling on those failures, she decided, and held on to her victories. Finally Raven ended the day's training and sent Angela on her way up the tree.

Several sore hours later, when Angela had reached the main platform, she saw the lights in their living area and could smell the food cooking. The prospect of food gave her new life, so she washed up and again met Raven in the kitchen area. Raven had assumed her human form; apparently, she preferred to use her feathers only for training. Dinner was incredible once again and Angela was able to eat her fill. After they were done and the dishes were cleaned, the two went out to the main platform and sat down.

"Explain to me what you experienced last night after I left you," said Raven.

Angela thought for a moment. "I heard ... everything. I heard what seemed like every sound in the woods. At first it felt like it was going to overwhelm me, but then something seemed to click and the sounds became easier to handle. I didn't need to focus to tune it all out. Even now I can hear so many sounds, but they are not distracting me like they did before or like they did in the classroom."

"That is really good," replied Raven. "Progress like that should have taken weeks to make, but you did it in one night. I'm not sure why, but you are progressing very quickly. Tonight I want you to focus on the sounds again, but this time I want you to single out each sound and learn everything you can."

"What do you mean? What can I learn?" asked Angela

"That is the question I will ask you tomorrow." Raven smiled, got up, and went back to her room.

Angela closed her eyes and let the sounds pour over her again. This time it was very easy since the sounds had been there all along. It didn't hurt to let them encompass her and she was able to embrace every sound. She began to focus on single sounds. The first sound that caught her attention was that of a bird flying overhead. She could hear the feathers cutting through the air and the wind moving around the bird's body. She focused on several different birds and found that tonight she could tell the size of the bird by the sound of the air it displaced. Angela then began listening to a bug that was crawling on the floor near her. She could hear all of its ten legs hitting the floor. 'Ten legs, huh,' she thought. She could hear it moving its legs and the scraping sound its shell made as it took each step. Just then a flash in her mind distracted her and she lost her focus on the bug. 'That was weird,' she thought.

She closed her eyes again and heard a small creature moving through the branches above her. At first she only heard it rustle through the leaves, but then she brought her focus in even more. She could hear its tiny claws scrape on the wood, and its furry tail move the leaves as it walked. She went deeper and heard its lungs expanding and contracting. She could hear its heart beating, and even its muscles contracting. That sound frightened her and she backed off to focus on other sounds in the area. She kept jumping from one sound to the next, realizing that she did not have to focus on only one sound at a time, but could listen to two, and then three. She could hear another bird cutting through the air and one of those two-tailed squirrels. She tried to focus on three creatures, then four and then five, all at the same time. She smiled to herself as the sounds began to form a picture in her mind. At first the picture was blurry and garbled, but with more focus it became clearer and clearer, and soon she could picture the surrounding area as if she had her eyes open. As the slight breeze moved through the trees, each leaf appeared in her mind. Soon she could see all of the tree around her in her mind, and everything that made a sound was easy to distinguish. She was able to rotate the picture in her mind and see other creatures moving near the tree as well. She backed off her senses and the picture grew. She guessed she was able to sense everything within fifty feet of where she was sitting, and most things within 100 feet. She opened her eyes and, painfully, got to her feet. Her legs had cramped severely while she was sitting there and she knew it was time once again to rub on the muscle cream and get some sleep. As she turned to walk back to her room, she saw the sun start to rise above the trees. She had been sitting there all night!

As she was walking back, she saw Raven eating in the kitchen area.

"Morning, Night Owl. I was wondering when you would get back. Tired?" asked Raven.

"Very, but it was amazing! I have to tell you what happened," answered Angela.

Angela proceed to tell Raven everything she had heard and seen, talking over several bowls of cereal. She thought she saw a look of concern cross Raven's face for a split second, but the look passed too quickly for Angela to be sure.

"Angela, that is amazing. You've achieved far more than what I expected and you're well beyond even my abilities; and you've reached this point in such a short amount of time. You are practically falling asleep on your feet now. Go get some rest and we will continue our training later today."

Angela did what she was told without hesitation. She staggered to her room and collapsed onto her bed. She couldn't help but feel excited over all she had accomplished in just a couple of days, especially because she knew that every task she mastered brought her that much closer to finding Emma and getting back home. When she laid down in the bed, she tried to relax every muscle in her body and in moments, despite the bright sun pouring into her windows, she was out cold.

Angela awoke just as the sun began to set, smelling the wonderful cooking from across the way. Angela smiled and her stomach growled. After rubbing on another healthy portion of the muscle cream, she met with Raven, who was waiting for her with some dinner.

"Are you ready to start training?" asked Raven.

"I am. I feel great," answered Angela.

"Looks like you truly are a Night Owl. I will meet you at the course."

With that, Raven walked to the platform and jumped. In midair, she feathered out right before Angela's eyes, spreading her wings and soaring off into the night. Angela could see in the darkness as if it were day time, but well after Raven was out of sight, she could still tell exactly where she was. The picture in her mind formed now without her having to put forth any effort. Just the sound of Raven's wings cutting through the air was enough for Angela to pinpoint exactly where Raven was. Soon other things moved into Angela's picture as well. She pulled herself out of her mind and began the long climb down.

Angela enjoyed being out at night, though right now it was surreal looking at the earth where the moon should be. She began to think about all her nights walking through the woods by her house. She always felt close to her Dad while she walked at night. Angela noticed that she was making pretty good time on this climb and then suddenly realized that she had feathered out! She was not wearing the special clothes that Raven had made for her, but it didn't seem to matter. Like last time, there were no wings.

Angela didn't care. She had finally figured out what made her change: the memories of her nighttime wanderings, thinking about her father. She truly was a night owl, and thinking about the night made her the owl. This time, the climb down went much quicker. Being able to see the tree both in her mind and with her eyes made her perception and dexterity even more acute. What had taken her two hours the night before took her only fifteen minutes tonight. She was able to jump from branch to branch with incredible speed. She was moving so fast that she was giddy with laughter.

Raven was shocked to see her so soon, but happy to see her in all her feathers. "You look great!" yelled Raven. "It is great to see you all feathered out. Can I assume that you figured out how to change, or did it happen on its own again?"

"Nope, I figured it out," answered Angela. "It sure did make it easier to get down the tree!"

"That's for sure. I didn't expect you so soon, but since you're here, let's get started."

For the first time, Angela was excited to run the obstacle course. She set herself at the start and took off like a bullet. She moved faster than she ever moved before. As she reached the first obstruction her extended hearing went into overdrive, and the picture in her head became clearer than ever before. She could sense every change in the course, almost before it happened. She flew through the course with no problems at all. The course seemed to sense that it was easier for Angela, and tried to become even more difficult than before, but it didn't matter. There was nothing that could slow her down. She reached the end where Raven was waiting and saw the look of disbelief on her face.

"If I didn't see it, I wouldn't have believed it. You ran that course faster than I ever did; you finished it even faster than my teacher," said Raven in complete amazement.

"Really?" asked Angela with a big grin.

"I know you are excited, but really, Angela, there is something more going on here. Not only are you progressing more quickly than you should, but you are progressing farther then you should. I have no idea why, but we better figure it out soon. Come with me. We're going to move on to the next phase of your training."

Raven led Angela across the glen to where the river widened. Angela took a good look at the area. The river was moving very slowly here, and it was deeper than she had first thought. There were over thirty poles jutting out of the water at different heights. She expanded her senses to the river. The water did strange things to sound that reflected in her mind. Fish seemed to move instantly from one place to another, and their size would change as well. The rapid-fire changes made Angela dizzy, so she drew back. The area was very beautiful and Angela made a note to return here with a camera. She had one camera left that still had film; her digital cameras had all run out of batteries days ago. The light reflecting off Earth shimmered on the water and lit up the entire area. It was nighttime, but even without her special eyesight she could see everything. Raven jumped and perched on one of the poles; her balance was perfect. She then executed a series of martial art movements, jumping from one pole to the next. Raven moved elegantly and beautifully, but Angela had a feeling that if she were too close, she would have been knocked into the water as quick as a flash. Raven jumped, flipped and landed next to Angela, who was still standing on the beach.

"That was incredible!" exclaimed Angela, "I have never seen anything like that!"

Raven smiled. "I would think not; that is a fighting style that you will not see on Earth."

"How come?" asked Angela.

"It was designed for people with wings," answered Raven with another smile. "It will take some time, but I am going to teach you how to do that as well, one move at a time." With that statement, Raven began slowly executing a series of moves and Angela followed along as best she could. Angela's new strength kept her from getting tired, but it took all her concentration to execute the moves perfectly. To Angela's relief, she and Raven spent the entire night on the beach. Raven apparently knew she was not ready for the poles, and Angela was thankful for not having to get wet. Finally, when the sun was beginning to rise, Raven stopped. The exercises that Angela had just learned had pushed her body to even more extremes than the obstacle course. She had stretched and held poses that truly taxed her muscles. Raven would not accept anything short of perfection, so Angela was forced to perform each move hundreds of times.

"Until today I would have told you that I would never hurt like I did from training on the obstacle course. Now I actually miss that pain," grimaced Angela.

"Let's find something to eat and get some sleep. I didn't get to sleep during the day like you did!" With that Raven spread her wings and took off towards the tree. Angela was happy about being able to change into her feathers, but she still didn't have her wings. She took off at a jog towards the tree and began her climb. She was sore, so it took her longer than it did to get down, but not nearly as long as when she climbed without her feathers. She found Raven in her human form cooking some food. Angela wasn't sure if it was breakfast or dinner, but she was too tired to figure it out. On the table was a container of the muscle cream, and Angela dove in. Raven laughed.

"Looks like you come more alive at night. Let's use that ability in our training. For now, we will train after dark and sleep during the day. After you clean up, please get some sleep, and I will wake you at sun down."

Again, Angela didn't argue. She was beat, and much preferred the night time. She headed off to her room to sleep.

10

ON HER OWN

Each day followed the same schedule; together, they spent hours practicing the different motions over and over again. Some of the motions required the use of long and short staffs for weapons. Raven kept adding different moves that · became more and more complicated and expected nothing short of perfection, so Angela practiced all the motions until they were perfect. For something different, they would break up the training with occasional runs through the obstacle course.

One night, after two weeks of the same schedule, Raven stopped Angela's training early.

"I want you to continue your training tonight. I have to run an errand tomorrow, because we are in need of some supplies. We could live off the land well enough, but it would take time away from our training to hunt and gather more food, and we can't afford that. I am going back home to get what we need," said Raven.

The two walked for a moment towards the tree, when Raven spoke again.

"I just wish I had more answers. There is no denying that you are different. What took me months to learn, you are picking up in only days. Your abilities are progressing further than I thought possible. I need to find out why," said Raven.

"Don't you mean 'how'? returned Angela.

"No, I told you that this place chose you, and this place is what changed you. I need to know why there is such urgency with your changes. I will only be gone a half hour on Earth, but in that time you will get more than two weeks' worth of training in here. We have accomplished much in a short amount of time, but you still have more to learn if we have any hope of helping Emma."

Angela had almost forgotten about Emma. She had a feeling that Raven had been purposely distracting her with this rigorous schedule, but suddenly the terrible feeling of losing Emma came crashing back.

"When are we going back, and what do you expect us to be up against?" asked Angela.

"We'll be going back soon. I want you to continue practicing your technique. When I get back here, we will take it up a notch and see what you can really do. As far as what we are going to be up against, I'm not sure. I just know that your friend in the woods is like nothing I have ever seen. I just got away with my life and I don't think I did anything more than annoy him." Raven grimaced.

Angela frowned, and entered her starting stance. Raven turned to leave and said, "Keep practicing and I will be back as soon as I can."

Angela did as she was told and continued through her entire routine. She tried to focus, but her thoughts kept going back to Emma. She wondered if Emma was okay. Raven was confident that Emma was all right, but Raven also knew that there were still too many unanswered questions for her to be sure.

After a few hours, Angela stopped training and set down her staff. She wanted just to sit and put her feet in the water. The water was cool and felt great. Angela would continue her training as Raven instructed, but she also decided that she was going to end her days a little earlier, so she could take some time to explore. She had been here for over four weeks and she had not seen anything other than the grotto and the area where she and Raven lived, and of course the side of the tree she climbed up and down every day. She decided that exploring the jungle might not be a good idea on her own, since she had no idea what lived in the surrounding area, and no wings to get away quickly if she needed to. The tree, on the other hand, definitely warranted some exploring.

Angela finished up her training, and after a quick bite to eat and a long shower she was ready to try to find out more about the strange tree in which she was living. Angela remembered that Raven had talked about exploring most of the tree in all the years she had been coming here. She was not sure where Raven had explored, but Angela figured she would start near her room and work her way to the top. Whenever Angela reached a platform that overlooked the jungle, she would stop and admire the beauty of the scenery around her. At one platform, she could see the sun beginning to rise, with deep pinks and oranges starting to fill the sky. It was a breath-taking sight that Angela never tired of. She could also see Earth in the distance, which comforted her but also made her feel homesick. Angela noticed that there were no other trees in sight like the one she lived in. She assumed there must be more somewhere, but couldn't see any even with her intensified sight.

Turning from the incredible colors in the sky, Angela continued to explore. Raven was correct: each area and room seemed almost identical to hers. Nowhere were there traces of anyone ever having lived here. The seemingly random pathways and staircases moved from room to room to room and they all looked the same. Angela worked her way upward for hours and realized that, at this pace, it would take her months to go into every room. There were just too many. With that thought heavy on her mind, she decided to sit for a minute, since she had never really stopped to admire the beauty of the tree. The huge leaves formed a protective layer that separated the inside of the tree from the outside. Occasionally, beams of light would penetrate the thick layer of leaves, creating dancing patterns of shadows on the floors and trunk. Throughout the tree, Angela found benches and tables scattered on every level. The tree had been designed so that the residents of each level could easily get to a platform quickly, but the aesthetic beauty of each floor was not lost on Angela. The pattern of the stairs and the rooms had a soothing effect, one that made Angela feel at peace.

As she fought back a huge yawn, while sitting on a comfortable wooden bench, she caught a glimpse of something out of the corner of her eye. At first she thought it was a shadow from one of the great leaves around her, but it moved in a way that could not have been caused by the wind, or even the gentle movements the leaves would sometime make towards her. She focused her attention and a picture of the area formed in her mind. She could see everything around her, but couldn't see anything that would move in such a peculiar way. Thinking that it might just be her exhaustion kicking in, she got up from the bench and continued on her way. After another two hours of seeing the same rooms over and over, Angela decided it was time to get some sleep. She turned around and walked back down to her room, keeping track of where she had finished exploring by counting the platforms on the way down. 'Tomorrow is another day,' she thought.

In the end, even though tomorrow was indeed another day, it passed the same as the last one had. Angela did her exercises and moved through her routines. She also took a round on the obstacle course for good measure. After she had eaten and cleaned up, she went to explore the tree again, coming to the same conclusion as the night before that each floor and set of rooms was exactly the same. She decided that unless she saw something that was worth further investigation, she would skip every other floor and just try to work her way up to the top of the tree. She smiled as she realized that Raven probably would not be able to explore the tree that way. During the time she had spent with Raven, Angela had come to realize how compulsive Raven could be about collecting. Angela kept finding small piles of similar stones in places where Raven had been. The stones were always pretty or shiny enough to be noticed, but not valuable enough to be kept. Raven just collected them. Even the items in Raven's rooms were always changed around and traded out for other trinkets from time to time. No, Raven would not be able to skip around. Her compulsion, even if on a subconscious level, would make her search each room. If her hunch were true, then Angela could see how it would take years to see everything. The tree was just that big. It would be like exploring an empty city and not missing one room in every apartment building.

Hours of wandering through the tree started to discourage Angela. She was hoping to find something different, something that would give her some answers as to why she was here, why this tree existed, or why she was covered in feathers! Instead of answers, all she got was tired.

Two more nights of the same meandering caused her spirits to become even lower. She sat down on a bench and looked at the table in front of her. The table had a pattern carved in the top, which reminded Angela of a weird type of checkers. She ran her finger down the pattern and up again. She decided that tomorrow she was going to try searching the jungle. It was getting late now; the sun would be up soon. The light reflecting from the Earth was cutting through the leaves, causing them to glow blue. She stood up from the bench and stretched, hearing the bones in her neck and back crack. She started to go back to her room, and again, out of the corner of her eye, she saw a strangely-moving shadow. This time, she turned in time to get a better look at where the shadow was headed. She broke into a run and saw it again. Though it looked like the shadow of a large bird, the picture in her mind showed her that there were no birds around casting any shadows. The shadow did not make a sound, so the only way to track it was to keep it in sight. Angela added a burst of speed.

She chased the shadow for ten minutes and initially thought she was gaining on it, but when she turned a corner on a level she had not seen yet, the shadow was gone. She stood still, trying to find the shadow again, but it did not reappear. Angela sat down to catch her breath. She looked around for a while, trying to get her bearings; she had not been here before and was not exactly sure where she was. She had been so focused on finding that shadow she forgot to pay attention to where she was going. She looked in all the rooms on the floor and found exactly the same uniformity as before. Since it was getting late and she was too tired to make it back, Angela decided that she would just sleep in one of these rooms. They were all pretty much the same anyway. She picked the closest one and made her way to the bed. The bed wasn't very comfortable, so Angela feathered out to use the feathers for extra padding and warmth.

Angela was woken up by the sun shining in her face. She didn't need the cream as much anymore, but she still woke up a little stiff every day. After some stretching and muscle-rubbing, she walked out of her room and stopped dead in her tracks. There was something different about this level. She wouldn't have noticed anything if she weren't so hungry, but there was no kitchen area here. Where that area should be was, instead, a breathtaking sight. The rays of the sun poured through the leaves like hundreds of small spotlights pointing to a stage. Angela could not tear her eyes away from the beautiful sight. Small dust particles and insects danced through the light, causing it to sparkle and glitter. It was the most beautiful thing she had ever seen. She found a bench and sat there, mesmerized, for quite some time. As the minutes passed and the sun rose further in the sky, the beams of light moved to mark its progress. With every passing second, the beams moved slowly towards each other and towards the trunk of the tree. Finally, the individual beams converged into one and shined directly on the trunk of the tree. As the circles of light became one, they lit up a carving of an owl on the tree. Angel walked slowly towards the carving, and as she approached, she saw that the owl carving was not just on the trunk of the tree, but on the face of a door. The door was carved in such a way that if you did not know it was there you could walk by it without ever seeing it. Angela was so excited. There was nothing like this anywhere else in the tree; at least, not that she had found. Just like the door at the school, this door seemed to pull Angela forward. She reached out her hand and pushed at the door, following it in as it opened into the tree.

11

TEACHER

After Raven left Angela at her training exercises, she passed through the door in the cave and emerged in the school. As before, Raven suspected that very little time had passed here on Earth since she had followed Angela through the door. Raven checked the clock on the wall, and then had to glance at it again. Time had moved slower here on Earth, as she knew it would, but not as slowly as it should have. In the past, a week on the other side would pass during an hour here. She expected it to be just over four hours later than it had been when they left, but it wasn't; it was almost eight hours later. She was confused; things were changing with the time difference and she had no idea why. For most of her life, the links between the two planets had been very predictable, so these changes were very unnerving for Raven. This new time difference meant that she needed to move quickly, since the time she thought she would have had now been cut in half.

There was someone she needed to see, and now she wasn't sure she would have the time. There were some answers that she needed to know, and she was hoping she could find them here.

Raven visited the grocery store and quickly gathered her supplies. She wanted to stop at her house, but now there wasn't time. She still had to make one more stop, and already a week had passed for Angela. She had no idea how long this last stop would take. Raven left town, headed south, and eventually turned into a long driveway that was off a little-traveled dirt road. Most people didn't even know that a house stood here, since it could not be seen from the road. Even in the winter time, the large pines on the property hid the house from prying eyes, and that's why Raven had chosen it. When she finally reached the house, after some time on the winding gravel driveway, she hesitated. Even on a good day, she could expect to be in here for well over an hour. She had 20 minutes, tops, before she had to leave.

She knocked on the front door and then let herself in. The house was small, but well maintained. The door opened into a small family room, which was decorated as if the house were in Arizona. Paintings of the desert hung on the walls, and Native American artifacts lay on every flat surface. The colors of the room were warm reds and yellows, which echoed the blankets draped over the furniture. Despite the clutter, everything in the room was clean and organized. Slouched in a chair was an older woman, who seemed to have fallen asleep while watching TV. She was dressed in a modified nurse's outfit. Instead of pants, she had on shorts and a short-sleeved shirt. Raven could feel right away that the house had been heated to well over 90 degrees. It was like an oven. The woman stirred and looked up, and turned down the news on the TV.

"Hello, Ginny. It's getting worse, isn't it?" asked Raven.

The woman rose to greet Raven and clasp her hands.

"When he's sleeping, I turn it down to 85 so I can at least breathe. I spend as much time as I can in the backyard, so I can cool down. You have come on a good day."

Raven was happy to hear that. "I'm glad, because I only have a little time today. Please come get me in 20 minutes."

"I will, honey. Can I get you something to drink? I stock ice by the bag now," Ginny chuckled.

Raven was about to say no, but realized that she was starting to feel really hot; a drink would probably help her stay cool.

"Yes, please. Whatever you have to drink would be fine," answered Raven.

"Okay. Go ahead in and I will bring you a soda," responded Ginny.

Ginny was a retired nurse. She had spent most of her years in the emergency room and liked it there best. She loved helping other people, and found that there was always a great need for help in the ER. Her husband had passed away years ago, leaving her alone, so she would work any shift in the hospital that was needed. One night, long ago, a woman came in to the hospital with a knife wound that was unlike anything Ginny had ever seen. The woman would not answer any questions about what had happened to her. Ginny told the woman that she would need to report a wound like this to the police, but the woman became very concerned and immediately spoke to her in a strange way. Ginny became instantly convinced that she should not call the authorities and that she should help this woman without further question.

Ginny fought this new feeling, and after a few minutes she regained her senses. Even though she knew she should call the police, she decided that this was no ordinary woman and that she needed Ginny's help. Ginny moved the woman to a private room and got to work. In no time at all, the woman's unusual wound was cleaned and stitched. The strange woman did not answer any questions herself, but she continually asked questions about Ginny. They chatted about many inconsequential things, but as every second passed, Ginny knew that she liked this woman and would be sad to see her go.

Several weeks later, Ginny was surprised to see the same woman at the hospital again, this time with several broken ribs. Ginny moved her back into the private room and tended her wounds. Again, the two talked and Ginny tried to convince the woman that she should call the police. This wound looked like the result of some type of abuse, and Ginny was very concerned. The woman again reassured her in that soothing voice that everything was okay. Their conversation shifted, and they began talking where they had left off during their last visit. Finally, Ginny did find out one thing about the woman: her name, Raven.

Over the next year, Raven would come to see Ginny at the hospital with one wound or another, and each time Ginny would try to ask her more and more questions. She never got a straight answer but that didn't dissuade her from asking; Ginny just enjoyed talking with Raven about nothing in particular. Raven always wanted to hear about Ginny's life and Ginny became very attached to Raven.

During that year, as the two of them became friends, they began visiting with each other outside of the hospital. Ginny stopped asking about how Raven was always getting hurt, since she knew she was not going to get an answer. She knew that Raven would not tell her any details, and would fluff off the injuries as simple accidents.

One night, just before her shift ended, Ginny received a simple text from Raven that said 'I need you,' and an address. Ginny immediately became concerned, since Raven had never contacted her like this before. Ginny grabbed a bag of medical supplies and went to the address listed in the text. She knew how to get there quickly, because she recognized the address as one from her old neighborhood. When she got to the correct address, the house door was slightly open, and she could see dim lights in the darkness. Ginny cautiously approached the door and whispered, "Hello ... is there anyone here?"

"In here, please," said a faint voice.

Ginny pushed the door open and hurried in. The house was beautifully decorated with many display and curio cabinets all around the room, but Ginny did not see any of that until later. She could not take her eyes off the woman -- at least she thought it was a woman -- lying on the floor, covered with black feathers and with two giant black wings sprouting from her back. One of the wings was bent in a terrible direction, looking broken and almost torn from the woman's back. There were other wounds as well, with deep gashes and terrible bruising. The winged woman looked up at her with desperation and agony in her eyes and passed out.

Though Ginny was in shock over what she was seeing, her training and compassion overtook her after only a moment's hesitation, and she wasted no time in beginning to tend to the creature's wounds. She didn't care what -- or who -- she was looking at: Ginny helped people, and that was what she was going to do here. She didn't know anything about birds, but a broken bone was a broken bone. After setting the wing, she sewed the tears in the skin one at a time. After several hours, she sat back to observe her handiwork. The woman was still unconscious and Ginny was grateful for that; if she had stayed awake, the pain from all that work would have been intolerable.

Ginny sat on the couch and rubbed her sore hands. She was curious where Raven was, and tried calling her. As she placed the call, she heard another phone ringing on the floor next to the couch. She picked it up and saw that it was Raven's phone. She turned on a few more lights and looked at the creature on the floor, this time focusing only on her face.

"Raven?" she whispered. The creature stirred but did not wake. "Is that you?" Though the creature looked a little like Raven, it also didn't. Ginny could not explain what she was seeing, even to herself. Ginny stayed with the bird-creature for two days before she awoke. The bird-creature opened her eyes to see Ginny placing a cold towel on her forehead.

"Don't try to talk," said Ginny. "You are going to need some water."

Ginny got up and got a glass of water for the woman, who tried to stir but couldn't move much, because everything hurt. Ginny had placed the woman on couch pillows spread out on the floor. When Ginny returned with some water, she said to the creature, "I'm sorry about putting you on the floor, but with those bandaged wings, I didn't dare try to move you to a bed."

The bird-creature looked at her wings and moved them to feel out her injuries. The wings looked stiff, but the bones had mended, so she folded them in so she could sit up.

"Please help me to my feet," said the bird-creature.

Ginny gently helped the creature rise shakily to her feet. Right before Ginny's eyes, Raven turned back into her human form. Ginny's eyes grew large and a look of wonder appeared on her face, but she wasn't able to say anything at first.

"Well, you haven't run for the hills yet, so I'm glad for that!" said Raven, as she sat in one of her arm chairs. She was still a little dizzy and her injuries still hurt a great deal.

"No, but it was close there for a minute. My initial plan was to patch you up and then call for help, but when I was done tending to your wounds I recognized something about your face. That similarity, plus your phone on the floor, helped me put two and two together. So ... I take it you're not from around here."

Raven laughed. The way Ginny could keep her cool in unusual situations was one of the reasons she liked her so much.

"Well, no, I am from Arizona, but I have lived here for a while." Raven saw the look of disbelief on Ginny's face and she continued. "I was born fully human just like you and everyone else, but ..." Raven hesitated. "I was changed."

"Was it some type of government experiment or something like that?" asked Ginny.

Again Raven laughed, but this time she laughed so hard it hurt. "No, my changes were from something else. I can't really tell you what happened to me, but what I can tell you is that I'm part of a long line of people that were chosen to protect something. We are given this form to help us do so. I am one of the good guys," smiled Raven.

"Well, I figured there was something strange about the injuries you've had over the last year, but not in my wildest dreams did I think this!"

The two women talked most of the night. Raven could not answer most of Ginny's questions, but she was able to say that there were other people out there that were trying to get the thing she was protecting, and that she was called to help when they caused trouble. That explanation was pretty vague, but it was all Ginny got. Raven told Ginny that she had been changed long ago, and trained heavily to fight those people, but from time to time the other guy would get in a good shot and she would need medical attention. After an exhausting conversation, Ginny made them some breakfast, then went home with the promise to check in on Raven the next day.

Since that night, the two had become trusted friends. Raven was never completely forthcoming with all the details of any altercation she had experienced, whenever she had to see Ginny in the hospital, but otherwise they were very close and shared almost everything with each other.

When Ginny finally did retire from the hospital, she became the logical choice for the caretaker that Raven needed. Ginny did not hesitate when she saw what Raven needed, and she took to the task very well.

Raven pushed open the bedroom door, and there in the center of the large bedroom, with his back to the door, stood a tall man in all-white clothes. Folded behind his back were two large white and grey wings. As he turned toward Raven, the wings unfolded and spread all the way across the room.

"Teacher," said Raven.

"Ahh, Raven. It has been so many years."

"I was here last week, Teacher," replied Raven with a look of sorrow and concern on her face.

"Really? I don't remember ... well, there are many things I don't remember nowadays."

Raven's teacher stood well over 6 feet tall, with handsome features that had only been attenuated with age. At one time, his feathers had been white and black like those of an eagle, but time had faded them to grey. When Raven met her teacher, she guessed that he was well over three hundred years old, but he never told her exactly how old he was. When she was chosen and then trained by him, she could tell that his mind was fading. Raven's training had taken place fifty years ago. His mind had wandered even farther away now, but he knew a great deal about Avaria, so maybe he would have some of the answers she needed. As Raven paused while she thought about the questions she needed to ask, she also thought about Angela, training alone on Avaria, so far from Earth.

Raven was instructed those many years ago to call him "teacher." One night, he told her that his name was Braden, but she was not to use it. At first, Raven did not like her instructor. She had been on her own and living on the streets when he found her. Raven was very accustomed to not having or living under any rules, but his teaching came with many rules and it took nearly two years until she appreciated them. Raven had considered having Angela call her teacher as well, but it didn't seem to fit. She could not put herself on the same level as Braden and give herself the title of teacher, even though Braden might disagree whole-heartedly.

The two eventually became close. Raven looked to her teacher as if he were her father, and in many ways he was. He was very encouraging but also knocked her on her butt when she needed that as well.

"Teacher, I have begun training the girl I told you about," said Raven. She hoped that her teacher would be able to stay connected to the present moment. She needed information from him.

"Very good. How did she handle the transformation?" asked Braden.

"Better than I did. She has taken to her new form and abilities as though she was born with them. She is learning faster than I could ever expect. Do you know why this would be? I am afraid of what is to come and I feel like there is more that I need you to teach me."

"Tell me, child, what form did she take?"

Raven was caught off guard and said, "An owl."

Braden's eyes flashed as if he were about to say something, but then he began to lose focus and he folded his wings behind him again. Raven knew that what he asked was important, but she had no idea why. She also knew that he was about to fade away again. He had a stone around his neck, too, but she could not talk to him with her mind as she could with Angela any more.

"Teacher, please try to remember. Is there something more about the times to come that you can tell me? Why is Angela so special? Why are things happening so quickly?"

"There has never been an owl," said Braden. "I knew that one day an owl would come, and then it would happen."

Raven straightened. "What do you mean? What would happen?"

"The reason for you; the reason for me. The time would come for us to ..." Braden's voice faded off.

"For us to what?!" Raven was practically yelling.

Braden's eyes clouded over and lost focus as he faded back away. Raven knew that asking further questions was no use; he had turned within himself and she knew that nothing but time would bring him back again. Time was the one thing that she did not have for this visit. It might be hours before he could talk again and he might not even remember that she was there. If there was more he could tell her, she would not hear it today. She knew she would need to bring Angela here as soon as she could.

Raven left the room and met Ginny in the hallway.

"That was fast. Has he faded again?" asked Ginny as she handed Raven a drink.

"Yes. It seems to happen so often now," frowned Raven.

"Physically, he is still as fit as a horse – well, a horse with wings, anyway -- but there is unfortunately nothing I can do about the dementia."

Raven quickly finished her soda and walked into the family room.

"I'm sorry I can't stay, but I have already spent too much time here. I have so many questions and I was hoping that I could find some answers."

Ginny looked concerned and asked, "Did you?"

"No, just more questions," answered Raven.

"You know I am here for you if you need me," said Ginny.

Raven hugged her friend and went outside to the car. She had to get to the school, and back to Angela as quick as she was able.

12

THE ROUND ROOM

Angela moved cautiously through the doorway in the tree and found herself engulfed in light, just as she had when she passed through the door in the class room. When she emerged on the other side, she found herself in a large circular room, easily one hundred feet across. She couldn't help but think that she was in a room made to look as though she was in the trunk of the tree. Equally spaced along the walls of the room were five large doors, each of which had a symbol that Angela did not recognize carved into the wood. Looking back as the door closed behind her, she could see the owl was carved into this side of the door as well. After checking to make sure that door was not locked, and that she could return to the outside of the tree, Angela turned to examine the room.

The floor was made of stone and covered with several area rugs. Each of the rugs depicted pictures of different animals, some of which she recognized and others she did not.

One rug in particular caught her attention because it showed people with wings! Finally! Some indication that there were people here, although she was not sure where "here" actually was. She marveled at the detail of the rug, but it bothered her as well. The people with the wings looked smaller and more human than she and Raven did, and there were no human figures without wings. Looking up, Angela saw that the ceiling was so high that it was hard to see the ceiling without using her enhanced vision. In the center of the room was a large round table with several odd chairs that had very high, narrow backs. She realized that the chair backs were designed to accommodate wings. There were also dozens of old couches and chairs with smaller tables in front of them placed throughout the room. Every square inch of the walls was covered in bookshelves, right up to the ceiling, every single one filled with books. In between and over the doors were also shelves filled with books; the room must have held thousands of books. Obviously, this room functioned as some type of library. The lighting in the room came from hundreds of lanterns that were either hanging from hooks on the wall or stood atop one of the tables in the room. She picked up a lantern and peered inside. She expected to see a flame, and wondered who lit them, and how they shown so bright. Angela was very surprised to see yellow stones inside the lantern, instead of a flame. The light that came from the stones was much brighter than any light bulb and together with the other lanterns lent a soft glow that blanketed the entire room.

Angela couldn't believe how many books were in the room; she figured it would take years to go through them all. 'Well, I'm not getting any younger,' she thought and reached for one of the books on the shelf in front of her. She opened the book and frowned. She guessed it had been too much to ask for English, or even recognizable letters. She put the book back and reached for another, and another, and another. The same language seemed to be in each of the first three books, all written in an alphabet that she did not remotely recognize. The fourth book was also in another language, but the alphabet looked different from the alphabet in the other three books. 'Great. Yet another language. I wonder how many different languages there are in here,' thought Angela.

Angela noticed something else spread out throughout the book shelves. Several small glass domes were embedded in the wall. Each one of them contained a small yellow crystal, but these did not light up.

After pulling several more books from the shelves, she gave up hope of finding one in English. The best she could hope for was one with pictures. She pulled at least ten more books off the shelves before she found one -- a book that contained pictures of people with wings. The book was thin, and only had a few pictures, but at least it was further proof that there had been some people like her here at one time. The question was, where exactly was she? There were no windows to look out and the door that she had passed through was obviously a portal. She walked to one of the other doors in the room and hesitantly tried to open it. It was locked. She could see a strange, star-shaped key hole. She looked around for a key, but there was none to be found. She tried another door in the room and it, too, was locked. As she looked more closely, she noticed that the doors were not only locked, but sealed tight; the doors didn't even seem to have any space around the edges. Angela changed into her bird form, since she figured she might as well get used to it, and tried another door. Just like the others, it was not going to open no matter how hard she pulled. She tried the rest of the doors with the same result. Only the door she had come through would open.

She decided that it was time to go back to the tree, and return tomorrow and go through some more books. Perhaps she would find one that had words she could understand, or at least some pictures that might give her a clue what this place was about.

Angela passed through the doorway and returned to the tree. She vamped up her senses and formed a picture in her mind. She noted where the door was and committed it to memory.

As Angela got closer to her room, she saw lights in the distance. Excitement overwhelmed her and she sprinted towards them. As she came down the steps, she could see a grinning Raven.

"Raven!" yelled Angela as she ran to her.

"Miss me!?" answered Raven as the two embraced.

"I was worried; you were gone so long. I expected you back much sooner," said Angela.

"I'm sorry; I came back as soon as I could. Have you kept up with your training?"

"I have, and I found something you are not going to believe," answered Angela.

Angela told Raven about the room and could tell that Raven was dumbfounded.

"You need to take me there right away!" exclaimed Raven.

The two of them sprinted back to the room and Angela had no problem finding the door again. Raven could not believe that this portal had been here for all this time and she had never found it. Together, they passed through the door and Raven was amazed at what she saw. The two of them spent the remainder of the night going through books. Raven was dismayed as she, too, found that they were all written in languages she did not understand, and the pictures that they did find were mostly of plants or trees. At least Raven recognized some of the plants from the jungle around the tree. It was a minor triumph, but it tied the tree more closely to this room. Raven spread her wings and flew to the top of the room. She found that there were many beams protruding from the walls. These beams gave her a place to land so she could read through the books in the upper area.

Finally, after sheer exhaustion set in, the two decided to call it quits. They needed to sleep, and Raven insisted on a full day of training before they would return again. After Raven tugged on a few of the other doors, the two returned back through the portal to the tree. Angela asked questions about home while they walked back to their rooms and was amazed to learn that Raven had been gone only two and a half hours, Earth time.

Angela finally reached her room and collapsed onto her bed. Raven told her that she would wake her later that evening, since the sun was now beginning to rise, and they would resume their training. Angela agreed, knowing that she would be ready. After one turn on her pillow, Angela was out like a light.

13

BUILDING CHARACTER

Angela awoke to a gentle nudge.

"The sun has set, we slept all day, and it's time to train. You didn't get soft while I was gone, did ya?" poked Raven.

"You wish!" answered Angela with a yawn. "I'm starving."

"I see that hasn't changed! I brought you some cereal."

Angela's mouth began to water. She had been craving cereal for days now. The milk had run out after the first week and the cereal had become dry and stale. Angela cleaned up, got dressed in one of the wraps Raven had given her, and joined her mentor for evening breakfast.

"I hope you have been practicing while I was gone, since it's time for the next phase of your training."

Angela smiled with a mouth full of food. After she had swallowed she said, "I have been. I am anxious to get started."

"Good. When you're done with the dishes, I will see you on the beach." With that statement, Raven spread her wings and took off for the grotto.

Angela had become very fast getting down the tree, but in the last two weeks there had been no hint of even one of her wings.

So, with a sigh, Angela sprinted for the platform and began her climb down the tree. When she arrived, Raven was waiting for her on the beach. Raven had changed to her bird form, but at the moment she also had no wings.

"It's time to see how much you have absorbed," and, with no warning at all, Raven attacked Angela.

The blows were swift and hard. Angela could tell that Raven was pulling her punches, but only a little. A good solid contact still hurt quite a bit. Raven continued to come at her and Angela did what she could to defend herself. The motions she had been practicing came to her more naturally, but Raven was still very fast and was excellent at improvising her attacks. Angela tried to predict what attack Raven was going to use next but everything she expected never came. It was always a combination that Angela did not expect, and eventually she ended up on the ground.

"Again," Raven would say and the melee would continue. Every so often Angela would land a blow, but Raven would block in a way that would lighten the impact if not completely deflect it. Angela began to get frustrated, and that was when Raven really delivered a good beating. Losing focus was the worst thing Angela could do.

Picking herself off the ground, and turning in time to hear Raven say, "Again," Angela went on the defensive. This battle went on for hours. During all the fighting, Raven would yell out corrections, and shout out defensive moves to get Angela going in the right direction, because Angela's increased speed and strength were no match against an opponent who had more experience and technique.

Finally, Raven said, "Enough." Angela collapsed on the beach. She had bruises on her bumps, and they covered most of her body. She looked up at Raven and was glad to see that Raven was rubbing a few of her own bruises.

"I hurt everywhere," moaned Angela.

Raven offered her hand, saying, "That's what I call building character!"

"I think I have enough character to last me a lifetime, after that beating," answered Angela.

"It will come. Give it time. As always, you did much better than I expected. Let's get something to eat and we can start again. This time we will use staffs."

"Great. I don't have any broken bones yet!" said Angela, as she rubbed her arm.

The two of them grabbed something quick to eat and started again with the training. Later, all Angela could remember from that session was how much more the staffs hurt. Every time she thought that her training could not get any harder, Raven would prove her wrong. She dove into the muscle cream before dinner as though it were candy.

After they were done eating, Raven cleared the plates away and sat back down at the table.

"Remember I told you how our stones tie us to this place? Well, it's time to show you what else we can do with them. I want you to clear your mind and hold the stone in your hand. Close your eyes and concentrate on nothing."

Angela did just that.

"I just heard you in my head! What was that?"

Raven smiled. "When we hold these stones, we can talk to each other in our minds. It is very convenient, especially because there does not seem to be a limit on how far away from one another we can be."

"So you can read my mind, then?" asked Angela.

"No, it doesn't work like that. It is just like talking to one another; you have to open your thoughts to me and I have to be willing to listen. I can't just tune into you and read what you are thinking. Now you try."

Angela focused and tried to project to Raven but she just couldn't do it.

"Nothing," said Angela.

"That's okay. This is going to take time. Your brain has been wired to communicate the old-fashioned way, but it will learn." They went back and forth at the table for an hour or so, and also on the way to the tower library. Angela was just not able to speak into Raven's mind. While they were going through the different books hoping to find something useful, Angela could feel Raven nudging her mind and she would try to reply, but she just couldn't project any of her words.

For the next week, the nights were full of sparring and book sorting. Nothing could be found in any of the books that they could understand, and none of the pictures they found gave them any real useful information.

One night, Raven finally heard a faint word from Angela in her mind. Angela became so excited that her super hearing kicked in and the picture in her mind came into focus. She was about to turn it back off when Raven realized that she could hear Angela perfectly. Not only that, but in her own mind Angela could 'see' where Raven was, and she 'looked' very different than all the other creatures around her. The figure in her mind glowed green and was incredibly clearly defined. She must have been able to sense her better because of the stone she wore around her neck. That night in the book tower, once again, did not turn up anything useful, so after hours of trying to read words that they couldn't make out, they turned in for the night. On the way back, Raven expressed how impressed she was with the progress Angela had made that night, but even Raven was surprised by what happened the following day.

The following evening, Angela again met Raven on the beach for another session of character building. After discovering how her mind's picture had helped Angela with communicating, she decided to integrate it into her fighting style. Now, not only could she see with her eyes, but she could see in her mind as well. Raven's moves became apparent well before Raven made them. Angela could not only defend well, she could now attack more and more. For the first time, that evening Raven jumped back towards the water and landed on one of the logs that projected from the surface. Angela followed her and brought the fight over the water. Now, Raven had the advantage of knowing where the logs were. Angela slipped a few times and landed in the water, but that did not slow her down for long. She was quickly up and ready for another attack. She could see that Raven was getting tired, which gave Angela a burst of energy. Raven jumped up in the air and, for the first time since they started sparring, she spread out her wings. The tides again turned in Raven's favor. Angela was fast, but Raven could move in and out with a series of flight patterns that gave her a definite advantage. Raven's new style change involved both ground- and air-based attacks, bringing in her wings when necessary. Angela would not give up. As Raven swooped in, Angela let out a blood-curdling battle cry and launched herself into the air...and it happened.

Two beautiful, strong, brown- and gold-feathered wings unfolded from Angela's back and pushed her through the air. Angela was so amazed at what happened that she totally lost her focus and forgot what she was doing. That moment gave Raven what she needed to send Angela spiraling down into the water. Raven landed on the beach with a huge smile on her face.

"Your wings!!! They are incredible!!" exclaimed Raven.

Angela pulled herself out of the water and shook her wings dry, a motion that came naturally to her, though she had no idea how.

Angela was speechless, but Raven could see that Angela was totally enamored with her wings.

"Now we are really going to get crazy with our training! You almost had me there. I was throwing everything I could think of at you but I just couldn't get in, and your counter strikes were faster than I could imagine! I must be some kind of teacher!!" laughed Raven.

Angela broke out of her awe for a moment to laugh with Raven.

"There isn't much more I can teach you as far as ground fighting now. We will still spar for an hour or so, but from here on out it will be flying and aerial combat lessons. You have a lot to learn if you are going to keep from getting tangled in a tree branch or telephone line."

Raven was right. Finally Angela did not have to climb the tree. With Raven's help and guidance, she was able to make her first flight to the platform without killing herself. Using her wings came naturally, but the technical aspects of flying still had to be learned.

For the first time, Angela wished there were mirrors in the tree. She could see her wings, but she wanted to see herself with them. The next morning, after she woke up, Angela practiced transforming. After having gotten her wings the day before, she could now transform with or without her wings at will. Angela was looking forward to her flying lessons, although Raven had decided that flying in the daytime would be better for her first couple of tries. Angela protested at first, but when Raven told her that they would not be the only creatures in the sky, Angela relented. She figured it would be best to focus on flying without having to look over her shoulder the entire time.

Angela rushed through her breakfast faster than ever. "Looks like someone is a little excited for today's lessons," laughed Raven.

"Before I found my wings, when I ran and jumped, it felt almost like I was flying because of how fast I could move. But to actually fly... in the sky ... with wings ... I can't imagine," said Angela.

"I understand how excited you are. Just be sure you listen very carefully to everything I say. After your lessons, you will be flying without a net, and the ground is very unforgiving. So your first few days of flying lessons are going to be very controlled."

Angela didn't care. She was tired of watching Raven fly back and forth out of the tree while she climbed slowly and painfully. Quickly, Angela cleaned the dishes from breakfast while Raven gave her some initial instructions.

"Your wings are not like those of regular birds. We do not have hollow bones like our smaller counterparts, which is why our wing span is so great. The muscles in your wings are stronger than any other muscle in your body, and they need to stay that way, so your exercise regimen will now include toning your wings. Because our wing span is so great, we have to be very careful of close-quarter flying. I will teach you how to do it, but we can't change physics. If our wings do not have enough room to capture air underneath them, we cannot get any lift. If we cannot get lift, then we fall. There is no way around that very simple rule, and that rule is one you can never forget. You also have something that I do not. Do you see those smaller feathers at the edges of your wings? Those are silencers. They will make the flapping of your wings virtually silent, which will be a great advantage. My wings are smaller and built more for speed than for soaring. I may be able to move a bit faster, but I will also make more noise."

Angela finished cleaning up the breakfast things, and Raven led her to a platform that she had not seen before. It was not like the other platforms, because it did not lead out to the edge of the tree, but instead it hung over a huge, hollowed-out section on the inside of the tree. Angela looked out off the platform and felt so small. The enormous area reminded her of a huge concert hall, with platforms like box seats scattered all over at different levels. About 30 feet below the platform were hundreds of branches that seemed to have a denser volume of leaves. These leaves overlapped each other at many different angles, forming what looked like a type of net. This area was obviously created for open flying within the tree. Angela stepped to the edge of the platform and looked down.

"I thought you said there wouldn't be a net."

Raven smiled, "You're going to be happy for this one. This area of the tree was designed for what we need to do. As you can see, it is large enough for open flight and also you'll notice the higher we go, the greater the wind. This area was perfectly designed to get you started with your flying training. There are three aspects of flight that you need to focus on. The first is take off, the second is sustained flight, and the third is landing. Today we are going to focus on landing. The platform is high enough that you do not need to get any additional lift to take off and the gentle winds at this level will help keep you up. What we are going to do today is glide in a circle and then land on this platform. Follow me and do not go out past the branches below." Raven laughed, "I have spent too much time on you to have to start over with someone else!"

With that remark, she spread her wings and stepped off the platform. Angela waited a few seconds and spread her wings as well. She could definitely see that her wings were longer than Raven's, and how that would be both an advantage and a disadvantage. The feel of the wind catching in her wings was exhilarating. After another pause, Angela stepped off the platform and leaned forward as she had seen Raven do. She realized that for a second she had her eyes closed and quickly opened them. Raven was right; the wind practically did all the work. She glided behind Raven as she executed a wide loop.

"That's fantastic, Angela, but focus on where you're going and how flexing the muscles in your wings influences your direction and height. We are going to loop a few times and then we will land."

Angela experimented with her new wings and followed every move that Raven made.

"Okay. We're going to land now, and as you come to the platform you want to be a little higher in the air. That way, when you're over the platform you can straighten up and gently drop to the ground as you let the air escape your wings."

Raven glided to the platform and, as she described, dropped to the platform as if she were gently lowered on a string. Angela tried to do the same and came in at too much of an angle.

"Go back around and try again. Don't rush it; take your time and get it right."

Angela did as she was instructed and on the third attempt she got the angle right. She stumbled a bit, but her landing was pretty good.

"Very good, Angela; you did a great job!"

"When I came in the last time I could feel that it was right for landing. It felt a lot like geometry class. I could see the angle in my mind and when I was able to get my body to follow that angle, I knew it was right for a landing," replied Angela.

"That's very good -- you have a flyer's instincts. Those instincts will make this training a lot easier. Let's go again," said Raven.

Raven and Angela practiced the looping and the landings several times. After their lunch break, Raven took Angela to the next higher platform in the clearing. At this level, the winds were a bit stronger, but because of the angle at which the wind hit the tree and the position of the surrounding branches, the winds were not overwhelming. The rest of the day's lessons were at this higher platform.

Again, Raven was amazed at how quickly Angela learned everything she was taught. Raven started to realize that when Angela had changed, she must have been given some basic knowledge of what she had to learn on a subconscious level; to Raven, that subconscious knowledge was further proof of the urgent need for Angela to be trained quickly.

The next day's training began in the grotto. Now that Angela could land almost perfectly under controlled conditions, Raven insisted that every morning begin with exercising and sparring.

"We spent yesterday on landing; today we are going to talk about takeoffs. Obviously, being able to fly is a huge advantage, but it will not do you any good if you can't get into the air. Takeoff points like platforms or cliff faces are perfect, but are few and far between. Unfortunately the most difficult takeoff is the one you will need to use most of the time, and that is from the ground. The trick is getting high enough quickly so that you can get your wings out and have enough room and air to get sufficient lift."

"So what is the trick?" asked Angela.

"Actually, 'trick' was probably a poor word choice. You need to jump really high and extend your wings up so they have room to come down. Let me show you."

Raven took three quick steps and jumped very high. Her wings spread out and Raven shot into the air. The motion was very fluid and graceful. Raven did a tight loop and landed next to Angela.

"Your turn," said Raven.

Angela turned and tried to imitate Raven. She took three steps and jumped. When she spread her wings one became hung up on the ground and folded under. Flying with one wing didn't really work, and she hit the ground hard.

"I would laugh, but that looked like it hurt," said Raven.

"I appreciate your consideration, because it did hurt," replied Angela as she brushed herself off.

"It's time to introduce you to the rocks."

Angela looked puzzled and followed Raven to a bend in the creek. Here, there were piles of boulders of all different sizes. Together, the piles looked like a small mountain about forty feet high. It was obvious that someone had built the mountain with the rocks from the surrounding area.

Raven reached down and picked up what looked like a leather harness. "Here you go. I made this for you."

"What is it? It looks like a harness," said Angela.

"You're right; it is a harness. There are times when you are going to need to carry something and still need the use of your hands. This harness will allow you to do just that."

Raven put the harness over Angela's shoulders and wrapped it around her back. Angela turned and stretched, checking her range of motion. The harness was very comfortable and didn't seem to hinder her movement at all. In the front hung a series of straps that seemed to allow for a variety of items to fit into them. Raven bent down and picked up a large boulder and placed it in the harness.

"There you go! This is your new best friend. Is it too heavy?"

Angela didn't want to show Raven any weakness so she replied, "No, it's okay."

"Really?" asked Raven and she picked up another rock and added it to the other.

"I bet it's heavy now," smiled Raven. Raven pointed to the huge pile of boulders, and said simply, "Climb."

Angela looked up and sighed. Ten minutes later she was at the top.

"Okay, good. Now fly down."

Angela spread her wings and jumped down. She fell very quickly and had to work really hard to stay in the air. The pressure on her wings was terrible. She struggled to get down and when she landed she dropped to her knees.

"That was really hard. My legs and wings are screaming!"

"Good! Do it again," answered Raven.

Angela had never refused any request from Raven, but she came close this time. Then Emma popped into her mind, and she climbed up the rock pile again, and again, and again.

After an hour of climbing, Raven added another rock. After another hour Angela could no longer walk nor fly. Her last landing brought tears to her eyes. She fell to her knees and collapsed to the ground. Raven got up from where she was sitting and walked over to Angela.

"Should I get the muscle cream?"

"Yeah, I think that would be good," squeaked Angela as she changed back to her human form and lay on her back, panting.

14

THE LIGHT AT THE END OF THE TUNNEL

Angela soon lived for flying, even when she was carrying a harness full of rocks. She took to it very quickly, and soon she could follow Raven through the most difficult maneuvers. The training with the rocks helped increase her wing strength as well as the strength in her legs. After two weeks of rock training, she was able to jump high enough to take off from the ground. Her wings were also much stronger and she could see the difference in her air speed and her maneuverability. She had an inherent ability to read the wind patterns and could use those currents to aid in her turns and acceleration.

When Angela had become proficient in flying through an open sky, Raven took her in and out of the tree's branches. Using her mind's picture and her natural talent with angles and reading the wind, Angela could navigate through the tree like a fighter pilot through a cavern. Even Raven could not catch her as she maneuvered at top speed through the maze of branches and leaves. Angela was able to pull her wings in and change the nature of their design as she flew, almost reshaping them. This reshaping made the wings easier to use in close cornering and so Angela's ability to bank and accelerate around turns was enhanced considerably.

After a particularly dicey chase through the trees, the two landed on a platform high up in the tree. Raven exclaimed, out of breath, "I didn't think flying like that was possible! Looks like the student is becoming the teacher!! I thought I would have the advantage within the tree but the way you brought in your wings was truly amazing!"

Angela was totally out of breath and all she could do was smile. She thought that Raven was an excellent teacher and didn't give herself enough credit.

Raven continued, "Tomorrow we are going to start aerial combat. Your takeoffs are excellent, your wings are strong and your maneuverability is unprecedented. We will start with theory after your morning exercises and then practical lessons after lunch. As far as the rest of today, I am giving you the afternoon off. What would you like to do?"

"How much of this planet have you explored?" asked Angela.

"I am not one for camping, so I have flown only as far as I can in a half a day in every direction. I have always come back by night fall."

"Have you seen anything cool?" Angela asked.

"Sure. This planet is beautiful, but covered with jungles and forests, at least within 8 hours of flying distance from the tree. There are very strange animals here, too," answered Raven.

"Can we go exploring today?" prompted Angela.

"Sure, but we need to be back here by nightfall. I do not want to sleep in the woods and you are not ready to fly at night," answered Raven.

"Why am I not ready for flying at night?" asked Angela.

"There are dangerous things on this planet, and some of them fly. When we have more time I will show you everything, but for now I want to keep you here in the grotto. I needed you to focus on flying to learn quickly, and that is exactly what you did. So for now, our exploring should take place during the day. Also, if you haven't noticed, there are not too many fully-lit airports with well designated landing strips. It is very easy to get lost when every single tree tends to look the same," said Raven.

"Okay. We can do our exploring during the day. I'll pack something for dinner," replied Angela.

"Excellent. I am going to clean up. I'll meet you in the kitchen area."

The two set off to gather what they needed for the trip and met up later as planned. Angela was very excited to see something beyond the grotto.

"You lead," Raven said with a smile.

"Great. Let me know if you fall behind," said Angela, laughing, and with a quick jump she burst into the air.

"Yeah, right!" yelled Raven as she followed close behind.

For the next hour, they soared over the jungle. The sight was breath-taking, but as Raven had said, soon all the trees began to look the same. The tree cover was so dense that Angela could not really see down to the ground. Her mind's pictures could sense the different animals in the area, but they were hidden too well to actually see. At first Angela was excited about her trip but now she was wondering if there was anything out here that she could enjoy looking at.

"There are a lot of trees out here," said Angela.

"I know. I can show you something cool if you follow me," replied Raven.

Raven made a hard bank and Angela followed. Soon they came to a river. Looking upstream, Angela could see where the smaller river that came from their grotto fed into this one. Raven turned and followed the river, then dove sharply to level out, ten feet above the water. Angela was right alongside her. The two soared as close to the water as they could. Angela could feel the spray from the moving water against her face. She had never felt so alive. She could feel each feather on her wings cutting through the air and it was exhilarating! For one brief moment of pure and utter joy Angela had forgotten about all her problems and become one with all that was around her.

"Stay with me!" yelled Raven, and Angela did. As they rounded a bend, the river opened and fell hundreds of feet down over the highest waterfall Angela had ever seen. Raven dove and followed the water down into the spray, where she pulled up and hovered over a large pool with water splashing down all around her. Angela was just behind her, laughing all the way down. She had not yet learned to hover like Raven, so she soared in tight circles, taking it all in. The pool, which was the size of a small lake, was surrounded by small beaches and then dense forests on all sides opposite the falls. The waterfall was not very wide, but the water still managed to roar like thunder, drowning out the sounds from the forest that Angela was used to hearing.

Angela soared to a beach near the waterfall and landed. Instead of following, Raven flew up in the air a few feet, curled her wings in, and changed into her human form while she dove into the pool of water. Though Angela was shocked, she immediately wanted to follow. She dropped her pack and her shoes on the beach, and jumped up. After two flaps of her wings, she shot into the air. At the pinnacle of her arch, she also changed into human form and dove into the water. It was cool and refreshing and still had that sweet clean taste. Angela absolutely loved the taste of the water here, and every drink was a treat to her.

Angela and Raven had some fun in the water for a while, and then made their way to the beach for some dinner. They talked and laughed and recounted memories of each other's past that kept them laughing through the entire evening.

"Well," said Raven, as she stretched out on some grass alongside the sand, "we should think about getting back. We are not far, but it will be getting dark soon."

"Okay," replied Angela, "but I want one more quick dip in the pool before we go."

"All right, but you are on your own. I'm finally dry."

Angela waded back out into the pool, and dove down towards the waterfall. The current was strong and the undertow would have been dangerous to someone who did not possess her increased strength. Curious how deep the water did go, she let the current take her down. Even in her human form she was able to hold her breath for a great deal of time; now it seemed like she didn't need to breathe at all. She saw all different types of fish. Some looked like the fish on Earth, while others were very strange, with what looked like small arms; some didn't even look like fish at all. As she followed the currents farther down, she could see a tunnel burrowing into the side of the cliff the waterfall fell over. She swam for the opening and looked in. She could see up ahead that the tunnel opened to the surface and seemed to lead to a wider cavern. With what was left of her air, she kicked hard and splashed through to the surface. The cave was large and opened to another tunnel that led farther into the mountain. Angela really wanted to explore further, but she figured Raven would be freaking out by now. Sure enough, the stone around her neck began to glow green and Angela felt a nudge in her mind and then Raven's thought, very loud and clear.

"What are you doing? You're scaring the crap out of me!"

Angela smiled and thought back, "Everything is fine. I am on my way up now."

She took a deep breath and went back out. Swimming against the current was slower, but not overly difficult. When she came to the surface, Raven was already in the air and about to dive in.

"What was that all about?! You scared the crap out of me!" Raven repeated.

"I'm sorry, but there's a tunnel behind the waterfall. The current is very strong, but I was able to get in and take a look around. It opens to air and heads into the cliff face. Do you want to take a look?"

Raven looked up at the sky and Angela could see a look of concern on her face.

"Okay, but only for a minute. It will be dark soon and we really need to head back."

Angela led Raven to the tunnel, and the two emerged to the open cave. There was no light at all, and although Angela could see as clear as day, Raven could not. Her eyesight was good in relative darkness, but not very good in the absence of all light. Raven touched the stone hanging from her neck and it glowed green, giving her enough light to see. Angela grabbed her stone and thought about speaking with Raven. That was all she needed to do to make hers glow as well.

Angela brought her senses in focus and her mind's picture formed. There was nothing else alive in this cave and she conveyed that to Raven.

"Good. I am not in the mood for surprises today," said Raven. They continued down the cave for quite a while and could tell that it was widening.

The floor of the cave was all loose river stone and crunched under their feet as they walked. The walls were dripping with water and covered in green algae. As the two walked by, the green light from their stones made the algae glow. It gave the cave a very surreal look that made Angela very uneasy. She continued to check the picture in her mind for any movement at all, but as far as she could tell they were still alone.

After walking for what seemed like forever, Angela broke the silence. "Where do you think it comes out?"

"I'm not sure. We have gone pretty far into the side of the cliff. I don't know if you noticed but the path hasn't been rising, only edging down slightly, so I don't expect to come out anywhere. We should probably head back," answered Raven.

"I agree," replied Angela.

They were about to turn around when Angela noticed that it was not quite as dark as it had been.

"There seems to be light somewhere up ahead," said Angela.

"How can that be? We are nowhere near the surface," observed Raven.

"Only one way to find out," said Angela.

Raven nodded and they continued forward. After several more minutes, the light became noticeably brighter. The tunnel widened and the ceiling rose to about twenty feet above their heads. Stalactites and stalagmites were everywhere, many of them having joined to form pillars that stretched from the floor to the ceiling. The pillars made it difficult to see what was up ahead. There were also huge boulders on the floor that made it hard to walk in a straight line. The rock formations cast eerie shadows that flickered along the walls and along the larger rocks. Angela imagined that she was walking into the mouth of some huge creature with giant teeth. As they worked their way over and around the rocks, they could finally see that the tunnel opened to a huge sprawling cavern. This area was clear of all rocks and the floor and walls seemed to be polished smooth. The cavern was hundreds of feet across and surrounded on all sides by stone walls that went as high as Angela could see. It was like someone had carved out a mountain and smoothed out the inside to make a giant rounded room. Placed in the center of the cavern was a cylindrical platform made of stone that was at least forty feet tall. Leading to the top of the platform was a narrow set of stairs, also carved of stone, that wrapped around the pillar, rising as they circled. The light was coming from the top of the platform.

Angela stood on the polished floor, looked around the cavern and said, "Does this count as a surprise?"

"Yes, it does," replied Raven.

The two approached the staircase and looked up to the top.

"Well, we've come this far. Do you sense anything?" asked Raven.

Angela focused on the surrounding area, forming the picture in her mind.

"As far as I can tell we are still alone. But the cavern is much bigger than I can sense. Look at the carvings in the pillar; I haven't seen anything like them in the library. They look ancient," remarked Angela.

"The big question is, do they say 'Come on, everyone, party up here!' or, 'Up here to a swift and sudden death!'" answered Raven.

Angela smiled. She loved the way Raven could easily break the tension in a stressful situation.

"I'm guessing that whoever went through all this trouble wouldn't have done it just to put in a dance floor," answered Angela.

"I would feel better if we feathered out," instructed Raven.

Angela agreed. She felt a bit more at ease as she felt her talons forming on her hands and feet. As the two reached the top of the steps, they could see more of what was on the platform. The pillar was easily twenty feet across, big enough for both of them to stand on top and spread out their wings. In the center of the platform was a stone table with two small pillars on each side. These pillars were only five feet high, and sitting on each was a large lantern with a larger version of the same type of stone that was in the lanterns in the book room. Set on the table was an ornate tablecloth with gold lettering that matched the stairs. In the center of the table were two small stone blocks about ten inches apart, and set across the top of the two blocks was a metal rod about twelve inches long and two and a half inches in diameter.

"What is that?" asked Angela.

"I'm not sure, but there are more of those letters carved into it," said Raven as she reached out to touch the rod.

"Are you sure that is a good idea?"

"We aren't Indiana Jones. What could happen?" Raven reached down to pick up the rod. "It's warm. That's odd."

"What do you mean, it's warm?" said Angela, "and who is Indian Jones?"

Raven smiled, "'Indiana.' I'll have to show you that movie someday. That's strange, though, the rod is stuck, and there doesn't seem to be anything holding it down."

Raven pulled hard on the rod again. It did not budge. Angela reached down as well.

"Let me try. Oh, it *is* warm." Angela reached down and picked up the rod without any problem.

"How did you do that? Let me see."

"It just came up. I didn't do anything."

Angela handed the staff to Raven and she dropped it back on the table immediately with a yelp. Until then, Angela hadn't realized they had been whispering.

"It shocked me!"

Angela reached down and nudged the rod with her hand. Nothing happened, so she picked it up again.

"It seems to like me better," said Angela as she rolled it in her hands. With a jerk, Angela suddenly looked up, and she partially unfolded her wings. Raven did the same. "Something is here, flying overhead."

"How big?" asked Raven.

"They're about the size of dogs, with wings," answered Angela.

"This is not good." Raven looked around. "This may be your first real test. The only thing I have seen here that is that size and can fly is not very friendly. It is very fast and has very sharp ends. One is not hard to fight, but I have never seen fewer than five at one time and they are very coordinated. In open sky they are easy to outrun, but in here, they will have the upper hand."

"There seems to be a lot more than five in here; there are too many to count and they are getting closer," said Angela.

"We have a minute. They will feel us out before they attack. They don't know what we are so they will be hesitant at first. They must have found this cavern and made it into some sort of nest. If that is the case, they must be able to fly out. We have two options: we can try to fly up and see if we can get out that way, or we can try to make it to the tunnel on foot. Either way, we are going to have a fight on our hands."

"If it's all the same to you, I would feel better in the air," said Angela, with a quiver in her voice.

"I agree," Raven assured her as she spread her wings. "They are going to come at us from every side and as fast as lightning. We will head straight up and hope for an exit. If we don't find something right away, we dive back down towards the tunnel. At first I will take the lead, but if we lose all the light then you will need to lead and I will follow you. Are you ready?"

"I am," said Angela with a stern look on her face.

"Okay. Now!" said Raven and she jumped straight up, unfolded her wings and flew. Angela was right behind her. After only a few seconds, Angela saw one of the creatures begin to approach Raven. Angela saw her slice at it with her talons. The creature moved away quickly, but not quickly enough to prevent getting clipped by Raven. It yelped and moved away. As Angela was focusing on the hurt creature, another one cut into her leg. Angela yelled and kicked out against nothing but air. Another one slashed at her side, and she yelled again.

"Remember your training! You are not that girl standing in the park trying to get your camera from a bully anymore!" and with that, Raven did something Angela had never seen her do before. She screamed, or, more accurately, screeched. The noise was so loud it made Angela's ears hurt, and then even her spine. Five of the creatures that were above them, moving into an attack position, suddenly veered away and lost control of their muscles. They writhed in the air and fell to the ground with five loud thumps.

Angela did not have time to ask what had happened, since two more were coming at her. At that moment, she realized that she still had the small rod in her hand. She wished it was bigger as she pulled it back to swing at one of the creatures. As she drew it over her head, the rod changed in her hand. Almost instantly, the ends extended and the rod grew into a long staff. From each end protruded a long thin blade. When it had finished expanding, the rod had become at least five feet long, with fourteen-inch blades on each end. Angela didn't think; she moved the staff with practiced precision. With inhuman speed, she cut through all the creatures that dared to get close enough. The creatures now saw Angela as the biggest threat, and moved away from Raven to focus on her. Angela sped toward the six new opponents. She could see everything in her mind's picture with incredible clarity. She could sense even the slightest muscle twitch, indicating which creature would strike first and how. She was able to anticipate every movement and attack from the creatures. When they were only a few feet away, Angela curled in one of her wings and rolled in the air, bringing the staff around like a bolt of lightning. The staff cleaved two creatures completely in half. Bringing her wing back up, she spun around and pierced another one with the talons on her foot, while bringing the staff around again to take out a fourth. Within two seconds, four were dead and the last two quickly decided that this meal had too high a price and veered away. Raven hovered in the air in absolute astonishment.

"Quickly, before they regroup!" yelled Raven with a look of complete and utter shock on her face.

Without a word, Angela shot upward like a rocket, with Raven right behind her. Finally, they got high enough that they could see another light. It was not bright, but at least it gave them something to head for. The light led them to another tunnel that was just wide enough for the two to fly through. Angela could sense seven more of the creatures following behind them. To their great relief, the tunnel opened up to the night sky. Angela whooped as she passed through the opening. The creatures did not want to follow them and stopped at the tunnel exit, realizing their advantage was gone.

Angela's adrenaline started to subside and she could now think about the creatures that had attacked them. Their bodies were covered in black oily feathers, but the wings were just like bat wings. Along the sides of each wing were pointed spines that were as sharp as razors. The long tails that they used both as rudders and spears were also covered in sharp tines. Their wide, flat heads had mouths that that reminded Angela of a Venus Fly Trap that her uncle once had, but these mouths had sharp razor teeth. In short, these creatures were like sharks in the air, with talons and wings instead of fins.

"Angela, I have never seen anything like that, and where did you get that staff? I was expecting to start your aerial combat training and instead I think you should start mine!"

Angela held up the staff and it shrank back down to its original size. Raven's eyes widened as she realized it was the rod from the cave.

"I don't know how I did that; I just reacted. The staff seemed to grow as I needed it. I also noticed that when it hit the creatures it not only cut them, but it seemed to shock them as well."

Raven looked around for the river and said, "Look, there is the pool where we found the tunnel. Let's get our bags and head back to the tree. I want to get another look at that staff without having to look over my shoulder for another Piercer."

"Piercer?" asked Angela.

"That's what I call them. After seeing their tails, you know why," answered Raven.

"This was the strangest day off I've ever had," huffed Angela.

The two landed by the pool and cleaned themselves off. It was dark now, but Raven wanted to get back. Fortunately, their journey back was uneventful. Angela was thankful; she was dead tired and not in the mood for any more surprises.

15
GOING HOME

Angela and Raven landed on the main platform. Angela had never been so happy to see the giant tree.

"I think we've had enough excitement for one day," said Raven.

"I agree; I am so tired," said Angela.

"Go clean yourself up and meet me in the kitchen area. We need to tend to our wounds before an infection sets in. Those things secrete a poison that we need to treat before too long."

Angela did as she was told, and had Raven treat and bandage her cuts. Raven rubbed a cream on each infected area that immediately took the sting away.

"This cream will make you drowsy, but it works very well for any type of infection. We are going to be bringing as much of this cream home as we can when we leave tomorrow."

"We're leaving tomorrow?!" asked Angela in shock.

"You have come so far in your training in such a short amount of time; I couldn't be prouder. There is still tons you need to learn, but I can't justify keeping you here anymore knowing that we need to get Emma back. If, after getting her back, you decide to continue learning about what you have become, we will come back. It is now time to figure out what is going on at home. Go get some sleep and we will check out your new toy in the morning."

Angela got up and swayed a little.

"I think that cream is kicking in," said Angela, as she steadied herself against the table.

Angela made her way to her room and laid down hard on the bed. She was asleep by the time her head hit the pillow. For the first time since she had arrived, Angela's sleep was interrupted with dreams. She was in the caves again, standing on the pillar. This time, the cavern was well lit and there were people in the tunnel. Angela couldn't really see them, because they kept coming in and out of focus. The people stood in a circle, as if in some type of meeting. The dream faded back out and Angela saw herself flying over a desolate land. This lasted for only a few seconds, but for some reason it really frightened her.

Angela awoke to Raven poking her in the side.

"Hey, easy on the poking," moaned Angela.

"You were dreaming, and I don't think it was of ponies and unicorns. You were pretty restless -- was it about the creatures from last night? They make for excellent nightmares."

"No," answered Angela groggily, "I dreamed of the tunnels, but there were no creatures; there were people who looked as though they were holding a meeting. The cavern looked different, too; there was more light in it."

"That's strange. Well, someone did put the staff down there, and you must have been fixated on that idea. We can think about it more later. For now, let's get ourselves together. I brought some fruit for you for breakfast. I wanted to take a look at that staff while you were sleeping, but every time I touch it I get shocked. Maybe when you get up, you can show it to me more closely."

Angela arose, cleaned herself up, and got dressed. When she came out of the back room, Raven was turning the staff with a stick, apparently afraid to touch it and get shocked again. Angela walked over and picked up the staff.

"No shock," observed Angela.

"I see that. For some reason it only likes you," frowned Raven.

Angela held up the staff so Raven could see the writing on the side. Raven could see clearly that the writing bore no resemblance to the writing that they had seen in the round library.

"How do you make it expand?" asked Raven.

"I'm not sure. Last time I just thought, 'I wish this thing was longer' and ..." before Angela could complete her thought, the staff expanded -- but this time, no blades came out of the end.

"No blades this time," observed Raven.

Just then the blades came out, and then went back in.

"How did you do that?" asked Raven.

"It seems that all I need to do is think about what I want it to do and the staff does it."

Angela tried experimenting with the staff. She made it expand to different lengths; she made only one blade come out, then two, then none again. Then she made the staff small again. Next, Angela tried something on a whim. Remembering how the staff would also shock the Piercers, she sized the staff to about two feet long and aimed it out into the sky. Just as Raven turned to look, a bolt of lightning shot out of the end. The bolt of lightning blazed out about 50 feet and dispersed into the air.

"I did not expect that!!!" yelled Raven, as she jumped back.

"I didn't either, but I felt something like that when I hit those Piercers.

"Anyway, what about you? That scream thing you did was awesome! What else can you do that you have not told me about?" inquired Angela.

"You liked that?" said Raven with a sly grin. "My voice is ramped up like your hearing. I can make it sound so melodic that I can nudge people into doing what I say. When I sing, it is almost mesmerizing. People that hear my voice are put in a trance and can become very susceptible to suggestion. And then there is my screech. I can change the frequency to do different types of damage, from simply stunning someone to ... well, to do more. I have never used it to that extreme extent on a person, though, only on a Piercer. Stunning people is usually enough. That is how I got out of the woods after you left that night."

"That is really cool ... wait a sec. Have you ever used that persuasive voice on me?" asked Angela.

Raven stared at Angela for a second and said, "Did I mention how pretty you look today?" and walked away.

"Yeah, that is what I thought," laughed Angela. "When are we going to go back?"

"We should gather some supplies before we head back. I will go get some muscle and infection creams, while you pack up some food. I like to cook with it when I'm at home. We will meet back here in an hour and then go to the library. I want to take some books home with us as well."

With that, Raven and Angela quickly got up and set off on their tasks.

Angela took one more look at the grotto before she took off for the tree. She knew that little time had passed back on Earth, but as far as she was concerned, she had been here for a long enough time to become very attached to this place. It was still hard to wrap her mind around it. She looked over at the obstacle course; it had changed again. She walked to the stream and took a few sips of the water. She decided to fill several canteens full of the water, since she was going to miss that the most. After one last look, she spread out her wings and took off for the tree to meet Raven. She had learned so much about herself and what she could do here. Even without all the changes her body had undergone, she had grown a great deal in this grotto, and as much as she missed Earth, this, too, would always be her home as well.

Raven arrived at the tree soon after Angela. She also had a pack stuffed full. After a quick trip to the library to pick up some books, they were ready to head home. When they landed by the cave, they changed back into their human forms and put on some normal clothes. They didn't want to draw any attention to themselves, especially if they opened the door to a room full of people.

"If my calculations are correct, we should be coming back through the portal a few hours after I came here. It should be around 8:00 p.m. at home. We need to go through at the exact same time or one of us will be waiting for quite some time before the other comes through," instructed Raven.

"I still have a hard time wrapping my head around that time difference. I can't believe so little time has passed at home when so much has happened here," said Angela, as she followed Raven into the cave.

It occurred to her that she had never gone back into the cave and couldn't remember anything about coming through it. That had been a pretty confusing time. The cave immediately opened up into a larger area, about the size of a classroom in her school. Along the wall were several doors, very similar to the doors in the library. Two of them had a glow around them as if there were a very bright light behind each of them.

"Which door do we take?" asked Angela.

"The first door is mine. It takes me back to either the school or my house. The second door was never lit before, so I am assuming that door is linked to you. I don't know for sure where it goes, but I am guessing it will take us to your house. We can find out later. You and I will be the only people who will be able to see it, just like the door in the school."

"Do you mean to say that the doors open up to different locations? How do they know where to open to?" asked Angela.

"That's a good question. They're linked somehow through the stone around your neck, which acts as a beacon when we are on Earth. I have found that no matter where I've lived over the years, I could always count on finding a door in my house and anywhere else I spend a lot of time. When you go through your door, just picture where you want to go on the other side. You can use either door, but the doors that follow you around will always take you back to the portal here. When you come through my door, you will always come back to my portal."

"Why are we going back to school and not your house?" asked Angela.

"We need to get my car," smiled Raven.

Angela laughed to herself. It was amazing how living here these last few months had changed the way she thought about things. She never even thought about a car.

Raven pulled her door open and the two stepped through at the same time. When they emerged on the other side, they were standing in a room full of people, with sunlight pouring through the windows.

16

THE GUARDIANS

If there had to be people in the room, at least there were tons of people. Everyone was too busy to notice Raven and Angela suddenly appear from nowhere. Even as the two started walking, with shocked looks on their faces, they went unnoticed. It helped that no one but Angela and Raven could actually see the door. As far as anyone else was concerned, Raven and Angela had slipped in from the hallway and were only noticed as they began walking. Angela's lack of popularity came in handy; no one really cared that she was there.

"This doesn't look like an empty room at night time," whispered Angela.

"You noticed that, too?" Raven whispered back. "Let's get out of here before people start asking questions. We need to find out what the date and time are."

The two had turned to leave the common room, when Angela heard her name.

"Angela? What are you doing?" said a voice from across the room.

"It's Mrs. Wren," said Angela. "This must be a yearbook meeting."

"Give me your pack and do your best to get free. I will get the car and meet you at the door," instructed Raven.

Angela handed over her pack. As Raven slipped out of the common room, Mrs. Wren worked her way across the crowded room and approached Angela.

"I missed you in class today ... and you look a little ... different. I would ask if you were okay, but you look fine. I mean, you looked fine before, but now ... I can't explain it. You just look different," said Mrs. Wren.

"Well, I hope I look okay!" Angela feigned surprise.

"No, no, you look great. Anyway, why weren't you in class today?" asked Mrs. Wren, trying to change the subject.

Angela was thankful that the conversation had moved away from how she looked.

"I'm sorry. When I woke up this morning, I was not feeling well. By the afternoon I felt better, so I came in for a half day," said Angela, not making eye contact. She was not really good at lying, but thought that was a pretty good answer.

"Okay. Was that Ms. Cray with you?"

"Yes. I was helping her move some photography equipment, and then she was going to take me home. I completely forgot about the meeting today. I'm sorry," answered Angela.

"That's okay. Please stop by tomorrow during your study hall, and I will fill you in on the meeting. Also, if you could ask Ms. Cray about Jane's photos, I would appreciate it."

"Sure. No problem," said Angela as Mrs. Wren turned to leave.

Angela left the common room and found Raven outside in her car.

"I was about to come and get you. How did it go?" asked Raven, as Angela climbed into the car.

"Mrs. Wren asked where I was today and then mentioned something about Jane's photos. At least I found out that we were only gone for a day. My mom will be worried, but not as much as if I had been gone longer. It seems strange: all the things that I thought were so important last week, don't seem to matter at all anymore," said Angela.

"You have to be careful of that feeling. We can only be who we are if we are capable of living two lives. Everything that was important to you then must still be important now. You just have other things to add to your 'important list.' It will get easier for you," said Raven. She was looking at Angela with the kindness that Angela had grown to love.

"Right now, all I can think about is getting Emma back. I will worry about the yearbook when she is safe." Angela was surprised by the authority she heard in her own voice. She could tell that Raven was surprised, too.

"I agree with you. We need to get some things from my house. You can call your mom from there," said Raven.

"If I go another day without checking in, she will be on the next plane home. That will only cause problems," said Angela as they pulled up in front of Raven's house.

After getting off the phone with her mom, Angela went upstairs to talk to Raven. She hated lying to her mom, but had told her that she had some type of 24-hour flu and had spent the time in bed. She said she had slept through her mom's call and when she got up, she had gone to school to catch the last few periods of class. After assuring her mother repeatedly that she wouldn't miss another call, her mother finally let her go.

Angela walked past the bathroom on the way to Raven's room and stopped. She looked in at the beautiful glazed-tile shower and felt a longing she never felt before. The tree was really cool, but the bathrooms there did not hold a candle to the ones here on Earth.

Tearing herself away from the shower with a sigh, she went into Raven's room in time to see Raven hang up her cell phone.

"Who was that?" asked Angela.

"In order to find Emma, we are going to need to track the person who took her. I only know one person who can do that. I was calling to make sure it was a good time for us to go see him," answered Raven.

"A good time? We don't have the luxury of waiting for a good time. We don't know what's happening to Emma, and you say that we need to check for a good time?! Time is moving for her now and we've already lost a day!" exclaimed Angela

"Angela! Stop and breathe; it is not like that. I wasn't asking for permission to stop by. You will understand when we get there. Pull yourself together and think. If there is only one thing you should have learned after all this time, it's the need for a plan. You cannot just fly off and worry about what might happen when you get there," said Raven.

The two walked quickly out to the car, and Raven pointed it in the direction of the old country road she had visited the last time she was home. When they pulled up to the house, Ginny was outside weeding her flower beds.

"Hello, Raven, I didn't expect to see you again so soon," said Ginny.

Raven gave her a hug and replied, "Hello, Ginny, I would like you to meet my friend Angela."

Ginny looked at Angela and smiled, saying, "I'm happy to meet you." Ginny came forward to give Angela a hug.

"Is he inside?" asked Raven.

"No. He's in the back yard. Head on back and I will bring you some lemonade," answered Ginny.

Raven and Angela started around the back of the house, and entered the back yard through a wooden arched gate. Angela was too focused on Emma to ask any questions in the car about where they were headed, and was shocked when she saw the back yard. The acre was completely enclosed by dense pine trees and other coniferous bushes. In fact, the back yard looked like a park, with beautiful gardens and ornamental trees cut through by paved paths that wound in many directions. There were water ponds and small streams carving through the landscape, all teaming with koi. Everything was so incredibly maintained it took Angela's breath away. All the natural beauty that she saw, however, paled in comparison to what came next. Standing in a small clearing of grass near the house was a man -- with beautiful white and grey wings spread out behind him.

"Is that? Is he? I thought ..." stammered Angela.

"Hush. Yes, he is one of us. He was, or is, my teacher. You need to be cautious near him. Please don't say anything unless he asks you a question," said Raven gently.

The two approached the winged man, and Raven said, "Teacher, I would like to introduce you to someone."

"I'm sorry. Have we met before?" said the man, curling in his wings.

Raven frowned. She had feared this development, because her teacher was suffering from dementia. For a normal human, the disease would be traumatic, but for someone with an unusually long life span, this affliction was devastating. There were days that were good, when her teacher's memory was somewhat intact, but there were other days when talking to him was almost impossible.

"Hello, Teacher, my name is Raven and I am honored to meet you."

"The honor is mine. Now if you will excuse me, I am late for my afternoon tea." With that, he turned and entered his garden.

Angela approached Raven, saying, "I'm sorry. I assumed by the way you were talking that your teacher had ... you know, died."

"In a sense, he did. Towards the end of my training, I saw signs of what was to come, but the disease has become much worse since then. My training took years, mind you, so the change was very slow. Eventually it got to a point where he could not live on his own, which is where Ginny comes in. She is a good friend of mine and the only other person here that I fully trust. She knows some of our secrets but only what she needs to know to care of my teacher. I was hoping that today would be a good day and we would be able to talk to him, but it doesn't look like that will be the case. He wanted to meet you, and told me that it was very important that he do so. Unfortunately, his good days are becoming few and far between," said Raven.

Angela felt her only chance to find Emma slipping away. With all the things she had learned, she still had no idea how to even start looking for Emma. In desperation she asked, "Would it be okay if I talked to him?"

"Sure. But please don't feather out. I tried that one time to make him remember, but even though he had wings at the time, he kinda freaked," instructed Raven.

"I will be careful," answered Angela with a smile. She approached Raven's teacher, who was sitting on a bench in the garden. His white robe wrapped around him like the clothes Raven had made Angela, though his robe fell down to the ground. She could see his age in his handsome face, but he still looked like a movie star.

"May I join you?" asked Angela, as she bowed slightly to the man.

"Of course. Isn't the garden beautiful this time of year?"

Angela sat down on the hard marble bench and looked around. Much of the garden was in full bloom. A small stone patio surrounded the bench on which she sat, and planted around the bench in different color pots was a large collection of flowering plants in shades of pink, purple and white. There were several fruit trees in this area, and each tree had a flower bed planted around its base, containing many flowers that she didn't recognize. A nearby koi pond contained blue-flowering irises, and brightly colored koi fish wove between the flowers. She knew that some of the plantings were not local to this area, or even to this planet.

"This is the most beautiful garden I have ever seen," said Angela.

"It is very beautiful, isn't it? I enjoy spending my afternoons here. Have you come to see the garden as well?" asked the Teacher.

"I have, and I have come to talk to you also," answered Angela.

"Really? Well then, we should be properly introduced. My name is ... well, I guess you could call me Teacher. And may I ask your name?"

"You may. My name is Angela," said Angela with a smile.

"Well, Angela, it is my pleasure to meet you," replied the Teacher, with a smile that brightened his entire face.

The two sat quietly together looking at the garden. Angela could not help but feel the urgency boiling up inside her, but she knew that there was nothing she could do but be patient. Angela noticed that Teacher also wore a green stone around his neck, but it was different from hers. Instead of a bright emerald color, Teacher's stone shone a dull green. Angela decided to start there.

"That is a beautiful stone around your neck. Where did you get it?" asked Angela.

"This?" Teacher's hand moved up and touched the stone. "I got it so long ago it is hard to remember," he said as his hand went back to his tea.

Angela reached up and held her own stone, almost out of habit. Without knowing why, she reached out and wrapped her hand around the Teacher's stone as well. As she did, the two stones glowed together, and before she could let go of either stone, a bright green flash momentarily blinded both of them. The Teacher stood up quickly and Angela slipped off the bench onto the ground. Raven was by their side quickly, and steadied her Teacher as he stood.

"What was that?" asked Raven.

"Raven, what are you doing here? What is going on?" asked the Teacher with a look of concern and surprise on his face.

Raven stepped back with her mouth wide open. She could feel the strength returning to her Teacher as he moved away from her grip to help Angela to her feet.

"I don't understand. What happened?" asked Raven.

Angela got to her feet and looked at Teacher. "I don't know," she said. "There was a flash of green light and then I found myself on the ground." Raven and Angela both saw that the Teacher's stone had returned to its original brilliance, glowing brightly.

"Did you say green light?" asked the Teacher.

"Yes, bright green," answered Angela.

"Very interesting," said the Teacher under his breath. "It was my mind, wasn't it? How far was I gone?"

Raven stammered for a moment and with a look of shock on her face said, "You have been fading for a long time. Recently, you have been, well, away, most of the time. I usually only get you for a few minutes every couple of days, and you spend the rest of your time in the garden, unaware of who anyone is."

"I see. That must have been hard for you. I'm sorry you had to endure that." He looked around the garden as if it were the first time he had ever seen it. "Raven, I can tell you have done all this for me. I thank you," said Teacher.

The Teacher then turned to Angela. "I think I remember a little of what Raven has told me about you. You must be Angela. It is time to tell me everything. If you are here, then we haven't much time."

"I am confused. What just happened? You seem to be better!" exclaimed Raven.

Her Teacher smiled and said, "I am better. It seems that Angela, here, has given my mind just the jolt it needed to get back on pace. We can look into how that actually happened later. There is too little time right now but I promise I will tell you everything I know when I can. Now, tell me about everything that has happened with Angela."

Angela started to grow frustrated as Raven recounted everything they had gone through since going through the door for the first time. She was glad that Raven's Teacher was better but all she wanted to do was save Emma and telling

Teacher about Angela's training did not seem to be getting them any closer to finding her.

Raven's Teacher could sense Angela's growing unease and reassured her, "We will find your friend. I just need to make sure we have everything we need to bring her back once we do."

As Raven was completing her tale, Ginny joined them. Ginny stuttered a bit as she tried to express her amazement about Teacher's sudden recovery, and then sat silently, watching Teacher, as Raven finished her story.

Finally Raven's tale ended and Teacher sat quietly for a second. Angela was afraid that he had faded away again, but he suddenly spoke, saying, "We need to go now. I will tell you what I think is happening on the way."

After Raven's Teacher changed to his human form, he went to his room to get different clothes. Raven pulled Angela into another room and gave her some clothes that were similar to their training clothing, but were made of leather. These clothes also had a special pocket sewn into the front that was made specifically to hold the crystals that hung around their necks. The pocket allowed the crystals to be used while concealing the light they emitted. The pockets, then, would allow the three of them to communicate and still remain unnoticed. Angela found several other hidden pockets; one worked very well for her new staff. Since there were more pockets in the pant legs and others in the back of the shirt, Raven seemed to want her to be ready for anything. When they were all changed, they climbed into Raven's car.

"Where are we going?" asked Raven as she pulled out of the driveway.

"We need to go to where your friend was taken; seeing that spot will give us a start on her trail. Hopefully, when we find her it will lead us to the other missing kids, too," answered her Teacher.

"From what I was told, Emma disappeared near my house," said Angela.

"Then that is where we need to be. In the meantime, I need to tell you what you are getting into. As I am sure Raven has told you, we are changed so that we can become a Guardian. We don't necessarily have to guard the planet, but the knowledge that is passed from one Guardian to the next. Unfortunately my Teacher was not able to pass on everything that was intended due to a tragedy that took her life suddenly. The loss of knowledge was horrific but some of what she had known she was able to entrust to me. There has always only been one Guardian; one to keep our information safe until he or she senses that his or her time is short, and then understands the need to pass on that information. That Guardian would then be guided to the next Guardian, and tasked to train that person just as he or she was trained and, therefore, to become the Teacher. The stones come into play at this point. The stones act as a catalyst for the changes that are to come. Then they serve as a link to each other and to our new home in the tree. Though there is much more I need to tell you about the stones, I am afraid there is not enough time right now. As I said before, there is only ever one Guardian, and I believe that is still the case. One of our oldest stories tells of a time when one would be presented to a Guardian, not as a replacement, but to be trained to be a Leader. That person would end the long line of Guardians and lead her people against a great threat. There are parts that I still don't understand about this story, but I will tell you that I believe that you are that Leader, Angela."

"A Leader of whom? And for what reason?" asked Angela.

"The story says that the Leader will take others into battle and overcome the threat that could destroy us all. It seems that whatever that threat is, it also knows about this prophecy. Like me, it believes that the prophecy is now coming to fruition and it is trying to stop the Leader from being found. Somehow it knew where to generally look for that person, but not who it would exactly be. My guess, and it is only a guess, is that it found many who it believed could be that Leader, and took them. Once you were finally discovered and it saw that you were protected, it did the next best thing. It took something precious to you so you would come looking. There are other stories that I have been told, but too much is missing from the retelling over the years for them to make sense. For now, we must assess this threat and see what we can do to defeat it," concluded the Teacher.

"How do you know the story is about me?" asked Angela.

"Over the past thousand years, one Guardian has passed his knowledge to the next and there has been no deviation until now. I cannot explain the remarkable changes you have undergone, and in such a short amount of time, in any other way."

Raven chimed in before Angela completely fell apart at the thought of all the responsibility inherent in being the Leader. "Teacher, there have been other changes that I need to tell you about later, but what I don't understand is why someone would go through the trouble of taking someone who only *might* undergo the change, without being sure that the change would happen. There must be something more to it."

"That may be true," answered the Teacher. "But for now we don't have enough information to know for sure."

"So you see Emma as bait?" asked Angela, her voice cracking. She wondered what else Raven was referring to, but did not care to ask right now.

"I think so," answered the Teacher. Angela could hear remorse and compassion in his voice.

"So if anything happens to Emma, it is all my fault."

"No. No one, including you, could have predicted any of these events. It is not in any way your fault," admonished Raven.

Angela wanted to believe her, but was having a hard time doing so.

"How am I supposed to lead against this threat? Last week, at least last week Earth time, I was worried about things like getting up for school and my homework, or photography class. Now I have to worry about saving two worlds? It is just too much to take in!"

"Angela, you are not going to be alone. I will be there every step of the way. I have seen how your training has progressed and, quite frankly, I have seen you do things that no one else could have ever done. You are smart and compassionate, so who better to lead us?" asked Raven.

"I am going to ask again, exactly whom am I supposed to lead? The two of you?"

That question fell on silence. Finally the Teacher spoke, "That is an interesting question that begs an answer. That is why I never really considered the story before now. A leader is nothing without a follower. Unfortunately, I have none to offer, but the fact that our tree home on Avaria seems ready to house many more people than just us has not been lost on me. Perhaps this library that you have found will shed some light on the subject. For now, let us focus on finding your friend."

Angela had more questions, especially about the green

stones, but as they pulled up to Angela's house, her stomach dropped. Her uncle was parked in the driveway, and the lights were on in the house.

17

UNCLE ANDY

"Oh, no," said Angela, in a dejected tone of voice.

"Whose car is that?" asked Raven.

"It's my uncle's," said Angela. "Mom told me he would be stopping by. I had no idea when."

"We don't have time for extended family," said the Teacher.

"Angela and I will take care of the uncle ..." said Raven.

"And cousins," interrupted Angela.

"... and cousins," finished Raven. "I respectfully request that you remain here until they leave. It will not take long."

With that, Angela and Raven jumped out of the car and took off at a jog toward the house.

"My uncle is very pushy. He is a good guy but tough to argue with," warned Angela.

"Silly Angela, I don't argue," said Raven, with a huge smile that worried Angela just a bit.

"My mom has grown quite attached to her brother. Will she be upset with us after you are done with him?"

Raven's smile grew broader, and she laughed as they got to the door. When Angela pushed open the door, she saw her uncle sitting on her couch, and her young cousins chasing each other around the house.

"Hey, Uncle Andy, what brings you here?" asked Angela.

Angela's Uncle Andy was five years older than her mom. They looked nothing alike; Angela often teased her mom about how she looked nothing like any of her other family members. Uncle Andy was very tall. He had been an athlete earlier in his life, but the years had packed on more fat than muscle. Luckily, he had kept most of his hair, so he still looked pretty good. Angela always enjoyed spending time with her aunt and uncle, but sometimes their kids could be difficult. Jessie and Jeffrey were the three-year-old twins, Mary was five, and Jason was seven. On their own, the kids were fun to be with, but when you put them in the same room, things usually got broken. Last time they had come over it had been a good day; only one lamp had been broken. Angela was pretty sure that her Aunt Tracy was at home ... asleep.

"You know why I am here, Angela. Your mom sent me over to check on you. Imagine my surprise when I got here and you weren't home. Where have you been? School has been over for hours," said Uncle Andy.

"I was with my photography teacher. We are working on a special project." Angela found it was easier to bend the truth than to come right out and lie. Angela had never been good at lying and didn't even try with her mom. Raven had told her that she had only a few minutes to get her uncle to leave before Raven herself would handle the situation. Angela had seen

Raven handle the Piercers and knew just how persuasive she could be.

"I'm actually on my way back over there now. I just had to pick up some camera equipment," continued Angela.

"Who is this photography teacher, and where does he live?"

Angela felt sorry for her cousins and the future they had with their dad, even now while one of the twins was spinning his brother in her mom's office chair. Uncle Andy didn't trust anything he heard. He was the most confrontational person Angela had ever met. Her mom and Aunt Tracy knew how to handle him, but Angela had always found it better to avoid any real discussions with her uncle. Just as Angela was about to speak again, Raven took Uncle Andy's question as her cue to join in the conversation.

"Angela," called Raven quietly, as if she thought Angela would be alone. Angela had always thought Raven was pretty, but when she walked, or, as now, glided into the room, she looked like a super model. Angela had no idea how, but it almost looked as though Raven had grown taller!

Raven stopped short as if surprised by everyone in the room and spoke. "Well, who are all these charming people? My name is Ms. Cray; I'm Angela's photography teacher."

Angela's jaw dropped, so she wasn't surprised to see Uncle Andy's drop as well. She could see both Ms. Cray and Raven in the woman in front of her. Raven's already stunning good looks seemed to be amplified ten times.

"What are you doing?" whispered Angela under her breath.

"I am just introducing myself to your ..." Raven looked at Angela expectantly.

"Uncle," said Angela.

"I'm charmed," said Raven, as she held out her hand.

Uncle Andy still had not gathered all of his senses to respond beyond holding out his hand. Angela then thought of her aunt and she kicked him in the shin. Andy came to his senses and started to 'pretend' cough to try to make up for his momentary lapse in, well, everything.

"Hi. I'm Angela's Uncle Andy," said Andy with an awkward look on his face.

"Well, it's nice to meet you. Angela and I just stopped in to pick up a few things and then we were going to head out again. I didn't think there would be anyone here waiting for us. What a pleasant surprise." Then Raven continued, but her voice inflection changed a bit. "I'm sure you were only stopping by for a quick visit."

Andy shook his head for a moment and said, "Yes, we just stopped by for a quick visit."

Angela knew that there was no such thing as a quick visit when it came to Uncle Andy or Aunt Tracy.

Raven continued in that strange voice, "I'm sure your kids will really appreciate the stop at the ice cream shop on your way home as well."

"I wish we could stay but we need to get some ice cream before bed time. Do you guys want to join us?" asked Uncle Andy, with more hope in his voice than Angela had ever heard before.

"I wish we could, but our project is due tomorrow. I would love to take a rain check," answered Raven with a smile that would make most people, Uncle Andy included, swoon.

By now the kids were all hanging on Angela. A couple of weeks ago she would have been on the floor from the weight of them, but this time she held them all up easily.

"I'll put these monkeys in the car," smiled Angela, looking at her little cousins. Though they were very destructive, she still liked having them around. Angela walked the kids across the front yard to her uncle's car. After she was done strapping and belting them in, she turned to return to the house. As she did, she saw Raven leaving the house, with Andy walking behind her.

It was very difficult to get Uncle Andy to leave super model Raven, but Angela finally was able to walk her uncle out to his car with Raven close behind. She said, "Please tell my mother that I am fine, and that Ms. Cray and I will be working on this project until late tonight. Let her know I will call her tomorrow."

"Okay, Angela," said Andy as he climbed into his car. By now the kids were all over the car fighting, having apparently undone all of their seatbelts and straps. Uncle Andy forced them back into their seats and drove off, waving good-bye as they left.

Angela turned after the car drove away, to see the Teacher standing next to her, holding something strange in his hand.

"What is that?!" asked Angela.

"I found this in your room. It looks like some kind of video transmitter."

"In my room?! I have never seen that before! How long has it been there?!" yelled Angela.

"I saw it through the window from the car, so I entered the house through the back door. I am not sure how long it has been there, but I had an idea that it didn't belong."

"You saw that from the car?" asked Angela.

Raven answered for her Teacher, "His sight is very different from ours, just like your hearing is very unique."

"Come with me," said the Teacher. Raven did so without any hesitation. You could tell that she and her Teacher had a bond similar to the one between Raven and Angela. There were no questions; just instant obedience built on mutual respect, admiration, and trust.

"I have searched the entire house and this is the only thing I found, but it may be just what we need. This device is still working, and I can see where its transmissions go."

As they walked behind Teacher, Angela looked at Raven. "How did he move so fast and search the house so quickly? And what was that super model look back there!?"

"As I said before, my Teacher is gifted with sight and speed. Not only can he see better and farther then we can, he can also see in different spectrums. He can also see heat sources and energy waves of all kinds. Let's just say he doesn't miss a thing. If he says the house is clear, it's clear. As for my new look ... well, a girl has to have her secrets," smiled Raven.

"I will have to keep that in mind," returned Angela as they followed the Teacher down the road.

"Look up ahead. I see something there on the sidewalk." Angela squinted, but didn't see a thing, even with her better eyesight. Instead she closed her eyes and opened her mind's picture. She couldn't 'see' anything, but where the Teacher indicated, she could see a slight disturbance in the air, like the blurriness seen rising from a scorching hot road in the summer. She would have never noticed it if Teacher had not brought it to her attention.

"I can see it, too," said Angela.

"Really? That is remarkable. We will need to talk about your second sight when we have more time," remarked the Teacher.

"I'm starting to feel a bit left out here," pouted Raven. "You mind telling me what you guys see?"

"I would, but a girl has to have her secrets," said Angela, while sticking her tongue out at Raven.

Raven punched her on the shoulder.

"It's a portal," answered her Teacher.

"A portal?" said Angela and Raven at the same time.

"Yes. It looks similar to the portals we use to get back to our planet, but this one seems temporary. After a certain amount of time, this portal will be gone."

"This must be how that creature took Emma away," said Angela. "How do we open it?"

"The same way we open our portals. The energy within our crystals should be more than enough to reopen the portal. I can tell, however, that the portal is decaying and will not be here for very long. You only have a few hours, on this side anyway, before it is gone."

"On this side? On this side of where?" asked Angela.

"I don't know. I also would like to have more information before we enter, but we don't have the time. We need to follow before we don't have any options. I am hoping that whoever opened this portal doesn't know that we can see it, let alone follow," said Raven.

"I wouldn't be so sure," returned the Teacher. "Your friend was taken so you would be lured after her. They want you to follow her. That's why this portal is here. I am guessing that you can expect to be ambushed when you pass through."

"What a ray of sunshine you are turning out to be," smiled Angela.

The Teacher smiled in return.

"I don't see any choices here, though," said Raven.

"Hold your crystals and focus on the door. That should open it enough to pass through. You will most likely not have surprise on your side, so focus on your training; that is where your advantage will lie. I will remain here. If this portal closes, someone will need to be on this side to figure out how to get you back."

On that note, the two turned towards the portal and grasped their stones. The green glow filled the area but nothing else seemed to happen. They looked at the Teacher and he nodded, "The portal is open."

The two stepped forward together and, in a flash, they were gone.

18

THINGS GET COMPLICATED

The two emerged on the other side of the portal and were very surprised at what they saw. The space was unnaturally dark and the rank smell in the air – a cross between burning sulfur and ozone -- was unlike anything they had experienced before. Grimacing slightly from the smell, Raven and Angela stood in some type of open-air area that reminded Angela of pictures of Stonehenge. Stone pillars all around the perimeter defined the circular shape of the area, but most of the pillars were broken and decrepit. Many had fallen and now lay in large pieces on the floor. In the center of the area was a platform with strange writing on its surface. They were standing on that platform now, so Angela assumed that this was the portal to wherever they were. Either it was very cloudy outside, or there were no stars here. Beyond the space the land was desolate. She suddenly recognized it from what she had seen in her dreams. Recognition made her gasp and catch her breath. Raven looked at her and Angela nodded. Angela closed her eyes and immediately opened her senses, focusing on the surrounding area. As the picture quickly formed in her mind, she could tell that for now they were alone. Strangely, she could not hear any movement. This was the oddest sensation she had ever felt. There was always something alive around her, if only an insect or a small animal for her to sense, but not here. There was absolutely no life or even a breeze to generate any sound at all.

Angela spoke. "We are absolutely alone. What is this place? It looks like someone moved Stonehenge and placed it in the middle of a barren wasteland. I would feel more comfortable with some feathers," said Angela.

"No, not yet. I want to seem helpless if we are being watched. No sense in playing our best cards this early in the game," responded Raven. "The question is, what way should we go?"

"Look over there! It's Emma's sweater! I should know; I bought it for her for her last birthday," observed Angela.

"Over there," pointed Raven. "It's a baseball hat."

"That doesn't look like Emma's. That thing must have taken the other kids that disappeared, too."

"There might be more than one 'thing.' I'm guessing that this is too big to be just one creature. I expected to track whatever-they-are into some lair near the city. The last thing I expected was a portal to another planet. This problem just became much bigger than I was ready for," said Raven.

All the confidence that Angela had come to appreciate and count on seemed to have left Raven. Something in Angela's brain seemed to click and she knew without a doubt that it was no longer time to look to Raven as her leader. It was time for her to take command. Just then something happened that caught her completely off guard. A distant voice in her head, not one from any memory or anything she recalled, sounded clearly in her mind. 'Good, Angela, it is time for you to realize your place.' And then the distant voice went silent. She knew it was more than nerves but she didn't have time to think about it for even a second now.

"Raven, we need to go. We will head towards the direction of the sweater. I agree that we should not fly, not yet. We do need to move, though; we are exposed on all sides here and can be attacked too easily with few ways to defend ourselves."

Raven looked up and saw something in Angela that had not been there before, and she also knew that is was no longer time for her to lead. She drew strength from Angela's words and demeanor. She composed herself and nodded.

Looking across the landscape, Angela couldn't help but feel discouraged. The ground was black and scorched. There were no animals, plants, or even bugs; only rocks and dirt. It was hard to see anything off in the distance since the ground and sky were both jet black, making it difficult to tell where one began and the other ended. This world seemed to come directly from a nightmare. Perhaps she could see some hills in the distance, but everything beyond those hills was a mystery. The sky was just as scary to look at. There were no stars, or anything else that would indicate where they might be.

When they were a short distance away from the portal, they could easily make out a well-traveled road leading away into the distant hills. There was no cover to help defend them from an attack, but at the same time there was not even the slightest structure to hide anything intent on an ambush. There was nothing but desolation and darkness.

"We'd better hurry. I don't like being out in the open like this," said Angela. Raven agreed and they both increased their speed to a sprint.

After what seemed like hours, they finally approached the hills that they had seen from the portal. What little light they had had when they first arrived was now almost completely gone. Angela was worried that Raven would not be able to see. Her eyesight was excellent, but not in the absence of all light. In better conditions, both of them could continue at this speed for much longer, but the road was now becoming difficult to traverse due to rubble and debris, and with no light, Raven would not be able to continue at this pace.

Raven stumbled. Angela stopped and said, "We cannot continue in the dark like this. I think it is time we changed our tactic."

Angela removed her staff from her backpack and put it in her pants leg pocket.

She also took out a flashlight and hid her backpack under some rocks.

"Give me your backpack, please, so I can hide it, too. It's time for you to feather out. I will turn on the light at the same time. It is going to be a lot easier for them to find us than for us to find them."

Raven thought for a second, nodded, and changed. Angela turned on her light and at the same time her senses flared! Where there had been nothing but desolation and calm, there was now a flurry of movement. As if they had come from nowhere, five creatures appeared in the darkness from a portal they seemed to create on their own. They were all similar to that one creature she and Raven had encountered in the woods near her house, though that now seemed like a lifetime ago to Angela. Three or four nets suddenly flew at them from different directions. Caught, Raven drew in her already-folded wings close to her body and fell onto her side. Angela did the same, as rough hands forced her over onto her stomach. Though Angela was tense with anticipation about what was to happen, she was deeply thankful that her staff was not found. Raven also preferred to fight with a staff, but since hers was impossible to conceal, the rough hands found it quickly. The stones that hung around their necks were well hidden in the special shirt that they both wore, so they would cast no light and remained out of sight.

Angela closed her eyes and thought to Raven, "Let's let them do the work for now."

Angela could feel Raven's approval. The two were bound with rough ropes, and each was thrown over the shoulder of a creature. The other creatures lined up in front of them as well as behind them. Angela waited for a flash and to be pulled away from this place, but it never came. The group of creatures started to walk into the hills, carrying their prisoners.

Angela projected her thoughts to Raven and the two conversed silently.

"Looks like their quick entrance was a one-way trip, since they are walking us back," thought Angela.

"I was hoping for a quick portal ride to wherever they are taking us as well. Whomever I am draped over smells worse than rotting meat," answered Raven in disgust.

"They didn't even give us a blindfold. I guess they figure that we won't ever be leaving so no sense in keeping the location secret," said Angela.

"Where would we run to? There doesn't seem to be anything for miles. And look how they move: slowly and mechanically. Nowhere near as quickly as the thing we found in your woods. Looks like they are in no hurry since I know they can move faster," said Raven.

After passing over the hills, their destination became apparent, and Angela found out why it had been hard to distinguish the landscape from the sky. Ahead of the slowly-marching group was a steep mountain range that slowly took shape through the gloom. After several hours of walking, the party entered a wide-mouthed cave in the base of the mountain range. On either side of the cave entrance stood a strange human-like creature holding a long pole with a hook on the end. Angela thought these poles looked like strange and awkward weapons. She was not facing the right way for a good look at the mountain, but what she could see seemed to rise even higher than she had first thought. After what seemed like more hours trudging through the cave, they finally emerged from the other side of the mountain.

What the two saw on the other side made them both feel sick to their stomachs. They found themselves on the edge of what looked like a military training camp. Thousands of creatures, the likes of which neither of them had ever seen before, looked to be preparing for battle. Some of the creatures were insect-like, while others seemed vaguely related to humans. Each creature seemed to come from a unique nightmare, and all were working hard. Spread throughout the area in front of them were forges with high fires churning out weapon after weapon. Most were melee weapons that were vaguely recognizable, but others did not look like anything Angela had seen before.

Spread throughout the camp were several buildings, comprising a makeshift town. The buildings were very simple and crude, almost like giant shoe boxes with holes cut in the sides for windows and doors. Most of them were all the same size and shape and only one floor high. Hundreds of these buildings stood everywhere, and they all looked to have been constructed out of some dirty black material. Here and there stood other, larger buildings that were surrounded by groups of the small buildings.

As Angela and Raven struggled to absorb the implications of what they were seeing, the two were thrown unceremoniously onto the ground. Once on the ground, Angela could take a better look around. She could see that the mountains surrounded the entire town. Ramshackle barracks stood in rows along one side of the camp; scattered here and there were other large buildings whose purpose Angela could not discern. In the center of the camp there seemed to be another portal, but this one was huge and looked unfinished. The portal under construction was large enough to hold hundreds of people. The idea of a huge portal was the most terrifying part of this town. Though its purpose was obvious, Angela wondered grimly where the other side of that portal would go.

Scattered among the forges for weapon manufacturing, Angela could see many areas where the creatures were training for battle, both in small and large groups. Each creature looked stranger than the last, but at least Angela didn't see anything that looked as though it could fly. Angela knew that the ferocity and the brutality that she could see in those training rings would never leave her mind. Just as she was about to communicate with Raven, something walked up to where they lay on the ground.

"Look what have here: a bird and a worm. Commander will happy to see you two. Put hoods on and them bring to cells!" yelled the creature in a guttural tongue. Angela couldn't believe that the creature could speak English even though it was clearly not his native tongue.

"How does he know how to speak English?" asked Angela.

"No idea. There is definitely something more going on here that we initially thought," replied Raven.

The creature vaguely resembled a man with a piggish face. His upturned nose ran with a black liquid that stained the fangs that did not fit wholly into his mouth. In one hand he carried a whip, and a long knife had been stuck through his belt. With a crack of the whip, the two had smelly hoods thrust over their heads and again were picked up and carried off to a nearby area, which Angela identified as a small cave. The path through this cave led downward and had many twists and turns, which Angela mapped and stored in her mind. Finally the two were again thrown to the ground and the nets and hoods were removed. After some shuffling, there was a loud clang as the bars to their jail cells were slammed shut. Within a few minutes Angela could tell that they had been left alone, at least for the time being.

Angela looked over at Raven, who was sitting up and brushing herself off. Before Raven could speak, Angela reached out to her with her mind.

"I am guessing that even though we are alone they are probably still listening. This whole setup looks pretty primitive but what got us here was not. I think we should play ignorant for now and only speak to put on a show," said Angela.

"Good idea. We need to find out where Emma and any of the other kids might be, and then see what we can do to get out of here. I assume that you also memorized the way out? Do you sense anyone else close by?" asked Raven.

Angela closed her eyes and again opened her mind. There were many other cells in this jail and she could tell that some were occupied. Some cells contained creatures that looked like the ones on the surface, but there were also two humans. They were each curled into a ball in the corner of their cells. She focused hard and was both happy and disappointed to find that neither human was Emma. The humans would certainly still need to be freed even if she didn't know who they were.

"There are two humans down here, though neither is Emma and they are in a different wing of the jail. I do know how to get out but we need to find out more about what is going on here. Let's play along until we can find some answers," answered Angela.

"I agree. There is much we do not know and I am thinking that there is even more we have not been told by my Teacher. He seems to have more knowledge now than he did when I was studying under him," said Raven telepathically.

"I noticed that as well. He was not surprised at all that there was a portal waiting for us. At first I thought he was just very cool under pressure, but now I think there is more to it," replied Angela.

"Even with everything he may be holding back, I don't think he suspected at all what we have found here," thought Raven.

Raven smiled. Raven loved her Teacher and the bond between them ran very deep, but she knew Angela was right. They needed the entire truth and right now Angela and Raven needed to trust each other if they – and the other humans -- were going to get out alive.

Angela looked around her new room, grimacing at the smell. She remembered driving past dead animals on the side of the road in the hottest of summer time that smelled better than this cell. These cages were built against a long wall and sectioned off by bars in ten-foot spans. In this particular wing, the cells were only on one side of the large room. The other wings had cells on both sides. There were enough cells here to hold at least a hundred prisoners, and more if they put more than one prisoner in each cell. The stone floors were covered with a wet brown sludge. She caught herself before leaning against a wall that was also covered with the same sludge. The conditions were subhuman, and Angela could not imagine spending much time here.

As it was, they waited for several hours. Eventually, an iron door clanged open in the distance. Metal-booted footsteps approached and a creature, followed by two guards, approached the cells. Quicker than Raven could react, the guard brought out a long staff and sent one end through the bars to Raven's chest. The weapon delivered an electric shock that brought Raven to her knees, knocking her to the ground, unconscious. Angela jumped to her feet, ready to change, but she heard Raven's voice in her head, "Easy, Angela, I'm just pretending; the shock was not that bad." Angela looked up at the stranger with hatred in her eyes.

"Good. I wanted to speak to you in private. I am happy to see that you have not yet been turned into one of those freaks." The creature pointed at Raven with a look of disgust in his eyes. "Although you humans are almost as repulsive."

The creature was tall, over seven feet high, with two horns protruding from each side of his forehead, curling back around his ears like a ram. His fangs made it difficult for him to speak clearly but Angela could make out what he was saying well enough since his English was surprisingly good compared to the other creature. Angela wondered again how they knew her language. His thick black leather clothes reminded Angela of medieval armor. She could tell by the way he stood, and the way his guards reacted to his every move, that he was either in charge or close to it. In his hand was a large mace, carved to look like a screaming human skull. The unique handle had a type of trigger, so Angela figured there was more to it than just a blunt weapon. He approached the bars so closely that Angela could smell his rancid breath. She was glad that her sense of smell was still normal; his stink was bad enough.

"You do not cower like the other humans."

Angela realized her mistake: she was not showing fear. The anger she still felt from watching the attack on her friend had not subsided, so she was unable to show any other emotion. Angela said nothing.

"I will see what we can do about that. Tell me everything you know about your feathered friend here. It will go easier for you if you just tell me now. How many more are there? What type of weapons do they have? I will ask her, but I can assure you that the questioning will not be pleasant." The creature finished his speech and stared at her with beady red eyes.

Angela wanted to speak, but was afraid of saying the wrong thing. His questions reinforced the impression Angela had formed after seeing the camp: the creature sounded if he were readying for war. Angela decided to tell him as little as possible. "She is the only one that I know of."

The creature continued to stare as if prompting her to continue. "I was looking for my friend when she found me. The next thing I knew we were here. She told me to trust her if I wanted to get back alive. That is when we were taken here, to this cell."

Without replying, the creature pointed the mace at Angela and a bolt of electricity coursed through her body. The pain made her body tense and crumple to the floor, her back arching as the intense pain continued to surge through her body. Finally, the pain subsided enough to allow her to roll over onto her side. Her lip was bleeding where she had inadvertently bitten it. Angela fought back the urge to attack the creature who had caused such agony, and instead cowered in the corner of her cell.

"That's better, human. Your story was a lie, but it was a start. We shall talk more later. Take that one!" he yelled to the guards, while pointing his mace at Raven. "I will question her next."

Now Angela's fear had reached a new level. Either Raven was lying about the pain or the staff the guard used hurt a great deal less than that mace. She was afraid that, once Raven was taken away, she might never see her again. Her plan of playing along with the guards was not working as she had hoped it would.

Angela got back to her feet after the creatures left, carrying Raven between them. She was very worried about what was happening to Raven, but she kept having a recurring feeling that she should just sit tight. After what seemed like forever, the guards finally came back. This time the jailer was with them.

"Take to the slave quarters. Take other two also, I tired looking at them. Tell them no try escape or next time more pain!"

The door swung open and rough hands pulled Angela out of the cell.

"I have to go to the bathroom," said Angela.

The guard cuffed her on the side of the head.

"You no speak. You are now slave, will learn place," said the jailer, as he nodded at the guard. The guard hit her again.

Neither blow hurt Angela at all. Her new body was very resistant to being hit, but she feigned shock and pain. The guard then pushed her into the other guard, who grabbed her and shackled her hands together and then covered her eyes. After another push, she began to stumble down the corridor. One of the guards disappeared from Angela's mental image, and Angela saw him heading towards the cells that held the other humans. She thought it now safe to reach out to Raven with her mind.

'Raven, are you there?'

'I am,' came a quick response from her mentor.

'Are you okay? Where are you?'

'I am none the worse for wear, although they are pretty good at convincing people to talk. I told them the same story you told them. I was only pretending to be unconscious, although it took everything I had not to pass out. That mace packs quite a punch. It looks like I am heading back to my cozy cell with a granite view. Where are you?' asked Raven.

Angela was so relieved to hear that Raven was okay that she began to cry. Though she couldn't help the tears, they fit in well with the perception she wanted to leave with her captors, so she let them fall. It was also good to hear her friend's humor again.

Angela responded, 'It looks like I have been promoted to slave. They are moving me to my new home as well, which must be the slave quarters. I will see what I can find out and let you know.'

'That sounds good,' responded Raven. 'Angela, there is something you should know. I can't be sure but I gathered from my questioning that there is another one here like us."

Angela was shocked. 'Another? Who, and where?'

Raven answered quickly, 'I don't know, but they kept comparing how I handled . . . well, I don't want to go into details but they kept comparing me to someone else. Keep your ears open for that as well. If there is someone else here we can trust, it could make all the difference in the world.'

'I will,' answered Angela.

Angela walked along with her captor, deep in thought. Hearing about someone else like them who had been imprisoned, and undoubtedly tortured, made Angela realize that the situation was getting out of control. She and Raven needed to find out what they could, and get out of the camp to regroup.

Finally, Angela and her captor came out of the cave. In her mind's eye, Angela could see that the other guard was bringing along two other humans. That group had not yet caught up to Angela and her guard, but she could tell where they were. The guard removed the blindfold and Angela followed him across the grounds. The slave barracks looked the same as the prison cells, except that these barracks had barred windows. The slave barracks were also very far away from all the other buildings; they stood close only to the entrance to the prison cave. There were two guards at the only door into the building, and, from what Angela could tell, the building was on the other side of the camp from the prison cells. The guard grunted at the creatures at the door and one turned and placed his hand on a pad next to the door. It was a surprising bit of technology, given how rustic everything else looked. The door slid open with a grinding sound. Angela was pushed in through the door as it closed behind her.

The first thing she noticed was the smell. Though it wasn't pleasant, it was purely human. Immediately, Angela opened the rest of her senses and scanned the room. The air was stagnant and heavy, making Angela start to sweat as she took in her surroundings. She saw one large room with what seemed to be a type of bathroom on one side with a makeshift wall of bed sheets, hung to offer some privacy. 'That seems very human,' she thought to herself. The black wood that was used to construct the building made the room seem very gloomy and depressing. It also gave off an eerie sheen. Against the shiny walls stood many cots, each of which was covered with a thin, dirty blanket. Some humans were lying on some of the cots. A table stood towards the center of the room with some boxes around it that must have been used as chairs. Two small video cameras had been mounted in opposite corners of the room. They seemed very out of place to Angela. As she was pushed into the room, two boys that she did not recognize got off their cots and walked reluctantly over towards her. One other person, however, did not move slowly but ran to her at full speed.

"Angela! I can't believe you are here! How did you get here? It's been so long since I've seen you!"

"Emma!" said Angela as she opened her arms to hug her.

Angela suspected that time moved differently here just as it had for her on Avaria, but she had no frame of reference to know how long Emma thought she had been away. Also, Emma looked different. She was taller, and even though she was covered in dirt, she looked more toned and muscular. Her hair had grown a great deal and it seemed fuller. The shape of her eyes had even changed slightly. If Angela didn't know better, she would think this was Emma's older, and prettier, sister.

"Emma, are you okay? How long have you been here?" asked Angela.

Emma looked at her strangely. "I am okay now, though they were not gentle with me, or any of us, when we first arrived," she said as she looked around at the others who had now circled around them. "They are looking for someone specific. They thought it was you, but if you are here, I am guessing it's someone else."

"But how long have you been here?" Angela asked again.

"I'm not exactly sure, since I don't know how many days I was in the cell when I first arrived. It seemed like I was there for two or three days but it could have also been hours. I do know that I have been working as a slave for almost three months."

"Three months?!" exclaimed Angela. "You have only been gone for two days at home."

"I was told that time moved quicker here, but I had no idea that it was that quick." Emma then said quietly so only Angela could hear, "We are always watched."

Angela again focused on the cameras in her mind. The sound that the electricity made as it moved through the wires gave them a bluish hue. Angela certainly hadn't seen any such technology in the cells.

Angela was dismayed. The goal was to find Emma and get her home, but they did not expect to find a place like this at the end of the portal. She expected to have to fight her way out but not against so many of those nightmarish creatures. Raven had had a hard time fighting just one! She still thought that she might be able to fight her way back through the mountain and get to the portal, but that would mean leaving Raven in the cell. She would not have time to grab Emma and then free Raven before attracting too much attention from the rest of these creatures. Flying over the mountain would also not be easy; the tunnel was her only chance.

But beyond that there was something else that Angela had to now consider. Emma was not alone. Angela had hoped to find the other missing kids and free them as well. But it played out in her mind much differently. There was no chance in defeating everyone and leading so many people out without someone getting hurt, or even worse. Angela was now faced with an even harder problem: not only did she have to save Emma, but there was no way she could leave these poor kids here with only vague promises of returning one day with help. No, she would have to figure out how to get everyone home safely and that would take some time. She would use that time to make a plan, but to also figure out what was going on here, wherever "here" might be.

Angela nodded and looked at the people circling them and said, "Emma, would you please introduce me to your friends? I have a feeling we have a lot to talk about."

The End